ALL THE WRONG

Places

G.I.F.T.D

W2E
CONCEPTS

For more info:
Write 2 Eat Concepts, LLC
1965A Morris Ave
P.O. Box #2228
Union, NJ 07083
Write2Eat2@gmail.com

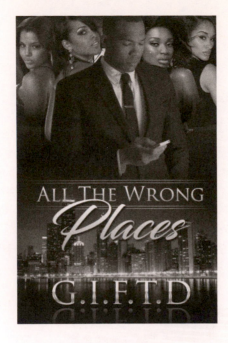

Boon

"I'd rather be with you, yeaaaa…said, yeah…girl, I'd rather be with you…" Bootsy Collins sang from the speaker of Boon's cellphone. It was Mela's ringtone, his girlfriend of six months. Daniel "Boon" Watson was 5'11 - average height for a man. He was not very muscular, but had a nice build on him, nonetheless. The feature that attracted ladies to him most, was his hazel eyes, which he inherited from his Panamanian mother. His tanned, brown complexion came from his African American father, a native of South Shore in East Chicago.

"Sexy, how is work?" Boon asked, as he answered his Samsung Galaxy Note 5.

"Boring, as usual." Mela's response was dry.

"Well, how 'bout we grab some White Zinfandel or a little Merlot, a karate flick, and some takeout? Let me bring you some fun, girl." Boon turned on his inner Casanova.

"I think I'll pass on the karate and takeout, but the Merlot don't sound half bad." Mela sounded less than interested, but Boon didn't make much of a fuss.

"Seen," he replied; a word his mom used as a statement to mean *understand*. "Do I pick you up or are you coming over?"

1

"I'll drive there. Look, my boss is coming. I'll be there later," Mela told Boon and they hung up the phone. Boon felt uneasy when the call ended. His thoughts raced back to the day he first saw Mela.

Mela and Boon had met at The Taste of Chicago, a yearly event that took place around the Fourth of July in Grant Park, Illinois. Jamela Howard, he soon discovered, was a graduate of DePaul University - just as he was. Upon seeing her, Boon was instantly attracted to Mela. She was about 5'8, with flawless, chocolate skin and a Coke bottle figure. She sat in the park with a few other women in lawn chairs, with a plate in her hand, glowing in the sunlight. Boon was with some of his teammates from the basketball team of Simeon High School, class of 1998. When discussing how they'd met, Mela always mentioned that she liked the confidence he showed by approaching her in front of her friends. As Boon gazed off into space, his doorbell rang.

"Who is it?" Boon yelled, as he got up to walk towards the door. He waited, but there was no answer. "Who is it?" He yelled, again, as he got to the door. Boon lived in a loft in the South Loop, located Downtown. With no kids, being the youngest of four children had its spoils. Not to mention, he worked as a law clerk at a prestigious law firm. He was currently in law school, studying to be a criminal defense attorney. Upon graduation, he hoped for a position as a litigator at the firm that currently employed him.

"Open the door, nigga, it's Yo. Got a nigga outside while you in there beatin' ya meat and shit."

"Hold up!" Boon retorted, snatching open the door.

"What's up, potna?" Yo reached to dap Boon up.

Johan Benoit, also known as Yo, was Boon's ace. They had known each other for the better part of the last two years. They met when Boon moved to South Loop after graduating from DePaul. Yo was 6'2, athletically built, and mixed with Puerto Rican and Haitian. He had long, curly hair that he wore, more often than not, in a ponytail. His skin was a golden-brown hue and he had chronic-induced, bloodshot eyes from smoking weed all day.

"Ain't shit. Come on in. Lemme go on and beat that ass again." Boon stepped aside to let Yo in the house, looking forward to the match. They both smoked weed and loved playing Madden and NBA 2K14 on Xbox One.

"Shiiiit! I bet me and Carmelo finna torch you," Yo bragged, taking a beer from the fridge, before sitting on the couch positioned directly in front of the 72-inch, flat screen TV mounted on the wall.

"Whatever, nigga. Roll up, I'ma be right back."

Boon went to use the restroom. Yo's phone rang just as Boon came out and went to the fridge to grab himself a beer.

"Shoot," he said, answering the phone. "Wit' my boy, playin' the game and smokin'. What up, tho'?" Yo spoke, while Boon set the game up. Boon could not hear the other party on the phone. "Oh, yeah? Hell yeah, we can do that." Yo listened for a second. "I'm in for the day. Bring some Trojan Magnums wit' you. Okay, cool," Yo said and ended the call.

"You know you supposed to buy ya own rubbers, right?" Boon quipped.

"Fuck these hoes. I ain't payin' fa shit. I take that back; I pay the hoes no attention." Both guys laughed.

They played six games. Boon won four of the six, during which, Boon had to warn Yo about his mouth. Yo was a sore loser and always resorted to name-calling and bragging about having more money and bitches than Boon.

"You pussy-whooped! That's the real reason you got one bitch!" Yo shouted, during one heated exchange.

"Mela ain't no bitch, dog! Watch yo' muthafuckin' mouth 'bout my lady, man, while you up in my shit too, nigga," Boon shot back.

Yo smirked and apologized for getting out of hand. "My bad, homie. That next ounce of Kush on me; matter fact, I owe you. You know I be takin' shit too seriously," Yo told Boon, as he got up and walked over to throw his empty beer bottles away.

"I'ma need that bud, too," Boon said, half-joking, as he dapped Yo up.

"I gotcha. Just come through tonight. If the music up loud, just come on in. You know I like my shit up loud as fuck," Yo said, walking out the door.

After a store run to get some Merlot and candles, Boon was back at home, doing some studying. He also drove to Jewel's on Roosevelt Road to grab a copy of *Think Like a Man* for him and Mela to watch. Although six months wasn't very long, in terms of relationships, Boon really liked Mela. He'd had relationships in the past, but none of them lasted very long. Women always told him he was more of the "homeboy" type. He was determined to work this one out. Bootsy Collins sang in his ear, just as he was slowly beginning to doze off, letting him know that Mela was calling.

"Hello," he answered, after fumbling to get the phone to his ear.

"Were you sleeping? I can wait and come tomorrow, if you want," Mela said.

"No, nah, baby; I was getting bored, reading this study guide for class. I'm awake; got Merlot on chill and a nice massage waiting for you," Boon said.

"Sounds good. I'll be there in about 15."

He ended the call, got up, and put his book away. Boon cut on some Tyrese, lit four candles, placing them in each corner of the living room, and set out the bucket of ice with the Merlot in it and two champagne flutes. He turned off the lights and sprayed a little Acqua di Giò cologne to erase the cannabis scent. Finally, the mood was set - and not a moment too soon. Mela used the key he'd given her to unlock the door, as he went to wash his hands and grab the massage oil that he had forgotten. He'd bought it from an adult, novelty shop. It was supposed to cause a fierce arousal for both males and females.

"Boon?" Mela called, when she stepped into the dimly-lit, glowing living room.

"Right here, sexy," Boon replied, setting the oil on one of the end tables. Approaching Mela, he grabbed her coat, scarf, and workbag.

"Boon, you didn't have to— "

"Sure I did. You deserve to be pampered after a hard day's work," Boon interjected.

He walked Mela to the couch and sat down beside her. Boon popped open the bottle of Merlot and began to fill both glasses.

"Boon, you are a great guy; handsome, smart, ambitious, and a great lover. I couldn't possibly deserve you," Mela murmured, as she reached for her glass.

"Don't say that. I dig what we got; seen? I can't wait to see what the future has in store for you and I," Boon said, in a voice he was sure would melt Mela. He slowly leaned in for a kiss.

"That's just it, though," she mumbled, turning her head to avoid the smooch. "I don't want that future."

Boon did not see it coming; just as he had not seen the majority of the other relationships falling apart.

"What… why? I don't understand, Mela." His heart skipped a beat, during his retreat.

"I mean… I like you, Boon, but it isn't strong enough to pursue anything more." Mela sipped her wine and sat the glass down.

Boon was baffled. "I am there for you. I give you money. We go out. What's missing, Mela?" Boon retorted, "You sit there and rundown how great of a guy I am, and then you stab me like this?" Boon's hurt reflected in his voice.

"I didn't want to hurt you, but I didn't want you to keep feeling like this was deeper than it is." Mela stood and went to gather her belongings. "I'm sorry, Boon. Someone will come along and love you how you want them to. It's just not me." She sauntered to the door, and just like that, Mela was gone.

Boon sat there dumbfounded. He halfway expected her to walk back in and tell him it was a joke. After 10 minutes had passed, he knew it was not so. He sat in the candlelit dimness for another 30 minutes, wondering what the fuck just happened. He finally got up to go to his footlocker by his bed. Inside, he kept pictures and small forget-me-nots of the serious relationships he had been in. There had only been five before Mela. Holding the empty massage oil bottle, he would put it in the footlocker, along with a picture of Mela.

"I need to smoke one. A nigga nerves is fucked up," he said to himself. Boon left the box open and went back to the living room to call Yo. *Damn voicemail.* A second call only went to voicemail again. "That nigga probably got that music blastin'. Lemme go catch this nigga before his company gets there." Boon rushed out the door.

*

It was a short trip to Yo's spot. Boon stayed on the fifth floor, in unit 571 and Yo lived in unit 365, on the third floor. Boon took the stairwell down to the third floor. Since he was a kid, he had a serious elevator phobia and avoided them - when he could. As he approached unit 365, Yo had been true to his word. Music, loud as ever, filled the halls. He paid his neighbors, handsomely, not to file complaints. "These bitches love Sosa...." Chief Keef was blaring through the walls of the loft. Boon knocked, but knew he couldn't be heard; hell, he barely heard the knocking himself. *The nigga said just come in*, Boon thought, and then twisted the knob.

"Yo," Boon yelled. He knew he wasn't loud enough. When he went towards the radio to turn it down, he saw shifting and moving through a small opening in the bedroom door.

"I'ma go see what this broad look like, since this nigga 'get so many bitches'," Boon mouthed, as he tiptoed towards the room.

When Boon got to the door, he could hear what he thought was flesh slapping against flesh. *They already fuckin'. Fuck that, I'm goin' in*, he thought.

He heard the woman moaning, "Ooh, Johan. Fuck me right...there. Beat this pussy, boy."

Boon pushed the door and stuck his head in. He saw Yo's back to him and the woman bent over the dresser.

"Oh…oh…oh, shit. You fuckin' the shit outta me," she moaned.

Yo's tearing this bitch up.

The girl put her hands on the dresser, and as she turned to look back at Yo, Boon felt his stomach balling in knots. It was Mela.

Harlots

Boon rushed out of Yo's house in a rage. He had always possessed the ability to think clearly under pressure. He ran up the stairs, as if something or someone had been chasing him. *But why*? He hadn't done anything wrong. All he did was go to get some bud, and then caught his very recent ex-girlfriend with a nigga who was supposed to be his homie. Boon got back to his loft, knowing that he had deserved none of the shit that was happening to him. He went to his room and sat on his bed.

"Fuckin' bitch! Triflin'-ass bitch!" he screamed.

As Boon reached for the last of a blunt he had lying in the ashtray on his nightstand, he tried making himself believe he did not care about Mela anyway. It had only been six months; and besides, she didn't give a fuck about him. The self-convincing didn't work. Boon lit the blunt and took a long pull on it. *That ho looked me dead in my face*, he thought, as he exhaled a big cloud of weed smoke from his lungs.

Boon stared off into space, as the pornography from Johan's room played in his head. He saw her making faces that she normally made with him. She'd never talked dirty for Boon the way she was doing for Yo.

"I just don't fuckin' get it," Boon said, as he sat the blunt roach in the ashtray to let it burn out.

He got up to grab a beer from the fridge and tripped over his footlocker that was open on the floor.

"Fuck!" he yelled, grabbing his toe on the way to the kitchen.

He got even more pissed when he got to the living room and saw the candles nearly burned out and the bottle of Merlot sweating on the coffee table.

"All this Romeo shit for a Jezebel," he chuckled, as he grabbed a Red Stripe out of the fridge.

When he looked at the beer, he thought about Yo.

"That bitch-ass nigga! Smilin' in my face, chillin' in my shit, and drinkin' with me. And gon' fuck my bitch!" Boon was getting in his feelings again.

She ain't my bitch no more though, he thought. *I wonder if that's who the fuck he was on the phone wit' earlier*. He blew out the candles and went back to his bedroom.

Boon woke up with all of his clothes on - even his shoes. He jumped up, as if he was running late for something, even though he was not due back at work or class for two more days. He was used to Mela waking him up to go have breakfast. He slowly came to his senses and the realization that he and Mela were no more. Boon got up to shower and brush the horrid taste from his mouth. Just as he did the night before, he tripped over his footlocker.

"You want me to look in there, huh?" he said aloud, as he stared at his throbbing foot.

He sat the footlocker on the bed and went to the bathroom to clean himself up. He planned to see why his feet seemed so interested in that damn metal box, after his shower.

Boon felt a bit fresher after his shower, even with last night's transgressions still fresh on his mind. He wrapped a towel around himself and went to sit on his bed. Right there, he poured the contents of the footlocker out. He heard his stomach growl and realized that, in the midst of the madness, he had skipped dinner.

He was thinking of ordering some hot wings and fries. "Where the hell is my phone?" he wondered, aloud. He found it in the living room on the coffee table, next to the bottle of warm Merlot. Boon grabbed his phone and twisted his lips, as he looked at the bottle. *Bitch*, he thought, walking back to his room.

His cell was dead, so he put it on the charger. He grabbed a pair of silk, Michael Kors boxers out of his drawer, along with a plain T-shirt, and put them on. Then, he slid on some True Religion blue jeans. Before he could find a sweatshirt to put on, he heard his phone buzz and sing a brief melody to notify him that it had powered on. Before he could get close enough to grab it, he heard Meek Mill's *"Ooh Kill 'Em"* start and stop, at least five times. It meant he had a few unread texts. When he did pick the phone up, he saw that he actually had six, unread texts, two missed calls, and one voice message.

Missed calls first, he thought, uncertain as to why he was nervous. The first one was from Johan at 11:40 p.m. The other missed call was from none other than Mela. *Bitch*. The call registered at exactly 12:21 a.m. *Voicemail next.*

"Boon, it's Yo. I see I missed ya calls earlier. I was...a little busy, my nigga. I still got that li'l package for you. Hit me up when you get this." Boon couldn't erase that shit fast enough.

Now for the texts. Message number one was from a co-worker named Damian Little.

Damian: Marshall wants files from the Woodard case on Wednesday.

14

Boon had already taken care of them. He only needed to turn them in. The next three messages were from Boon's oldest brother, Donovan. All of Donovan's messages were to remind Boon of their mom's surprise party in Las Vegas next weekend. Every year since Boon graduated college, he and his siblings threw their mom a surprise party somewhere different. Boon chose Vegas this year. The last two messages were from Mela.

Mela: I saw u see me and I'm ashamed. As a woman and as your ex. Plz forgive me and let me make it up 2 u

It had Boon rather taken aback and uncertain as to how he should react.

Mela: I still have my key, Boon. Will you be there at 9 p.m. sharp? Plz say u still want me...

Boon was confused, but didn't respond to Mela or Yo's messages. Instead, he texted Damian, "done", as it pertained to the Woodard case files and then texted Donovan.

Boon: Cool. see u guys at Mom's Friday.

He stuffed the contents from the footlocker back in it, locked it, and slid it back under his bed. He was hungry, horny, and heavy with confusion. *A couple jalapeño dogs, a large Coke, and some chili fries should do the trick*, he thought, as he rushed to put on a sweatshirt, coat, scarf, and skully. Chicago was colder than a hooker's heart in winter. He grabbed his phone and keys and headed down to his car.

Boon pulled out of the covered parking garage, after warming up his 2013 Dodge Challenger. It was fire engine red, with a deep cherry red interior, 24-inch Forges, and three 12's in the trunk. He put on his Rich Homie Quan CD and went to search for those hot dogs. Boon looked in his rearview and saw himself in the mirror. "Boy, you know you can do better than these ratchet-ass hoes," he said to his reflection, as he slid through traffic. Finally, he found a hot dog stand that didn't have an outrageous waiting line and pulled up. There were only four people in front of him, and one of them had ordered and was already paying for their food.

"I'd rather be with you, yeaa..." his phone began to ring, and of course, it was Mela. He sent her to voicemail.

"What you know about that, young blood?" asked the Sherman Helmsley look-alike in front of Boon.

"Plenty. I wish I didn't right now, though." *Really, I think it's time for a new city*, he thought, as it was his turn to step up and order.

"Lemme get three jalapeño and chili dogs, large fries, and large Coke." Boon could really eat about four or five dogs right now, but he didn't want the gas behind it.

"Nice car. When can I ride wit' you?" asked the pretty girl who took his order.

"Lemme think about it," he replied.

Minutes later, his food was ready and he stepped up to get it. "$8.65, sir," the pretty cashier said.

Boon handed her a 20. "Keep the change." He headed for the car.

"You thought about it yet?" the cashier asked, as he fumbled with the car keys.

"I'm good. You woulda been on some mo' shit if I didn't have this car," he said, as he got in and headed home. Mela had called at least three more times, since he had ordered his food. *I'ma change that ringtone when I get home*.

Boon successfully changed Mela's ringtone to Future's "These Bitches Ain't Shit", ate all of his food and had his brother, Drakus, bring him an ounce of Kush from K-Town, on the West Side of Chicago. Boon studied for an hour after he'd eaten, smoked a blunt, and was watching *Friday After Next* in his bedroom until he fell asleep. For the umpteenth time, he dreamt of his high school sweetheart, Curelle Dorsey, whom

17

everybody called CiCi. In his dreams, Boon always romanced and flattered CiCi, but he never had sex with her in them or in reality.

In this particular dream though, CiCi had kissed Boon from his lips to his length. It felt all too real. "Ooh shit," he felt a moan escape him. CiCi was full-fledge bobbing now, and it was waking Boon from his sleep; it was that good. However, he wasn't sleep anymore, but the feeling didn't stop. "Oh fuck…" he groaned, as he looked down to find the source of the great warmth damn near swallowing his penis.

"Mmm," Mela moaned, as she relentlessly sucked Boon's manhood.

"Oh shit, girl. Oh, I'm 'bout to...oh fuuuck!" Mela kept sucking, as Boon's juice spewed into her mouth. Boon's whole body jerked, as she did the one thing she swore she would never do— swallow. Boon was fighting fatigue, but would soon lose and fall fast asleep.

"Ooh… kill 'em, Ooh… kill 'em!" Meek Mill rapped and made Boon jump up from his sleep. He knew he had been awakened this morning once before, but he'd gone back to sleep. But for how long? He grabbed his phone to read the incoming text.

Mela: I deserved the new ringtone. Bt u gonna miss me more than I'ma miss u. Bet that.

Man, this ho deranged. He started to text back and chump the bitch off, but instead, he hit her with something different.

Boon: Yeah, but until then, lemme get my key tho'

Boon was glad to have dreamed about CiCi, but damn, Mela could suck a watermelon through a water hose. He got up off the bed and grabbed his footlocker from under it. Now, finally, he'd go through the box.

He dumped the box's contents on his bed and sat the box on the floor. There were five, different Ziploc bags; one for each girlfriend past. He separated them in sequential order, starting with Mela's duck-ass, and working his way backwards. He didn't want to think about that slut right now, so he moved her pictures and memories to the side.

The first picture was of Tatiyana "Taz" Lopes. She was by far the most beautiful, as well as the vainest of his exes. She was Puerto Rican and black, 5'3, 135 pounds, high yellow, and had green eyes. Boon was looking at a picture of him and her kissing at Mardi Gras 2011 in New Orleans. Tatiyana got her nickname, Taz, from being crazy and fighting a lot throughout middle and high school. Tatiyana left Boon, three months before graduation, to be with a star, NFL cornerback named Todd Cambridge. She told Boon, "When your money get as long as his, hit me up." *All I got was some pussy*, Boon thought. He tossed her Ziploc aside.

The next bag he came to had ultrasound pictures in it, and instantly made Boon irate. "This ho!" he gritted.

The contents of that bag belonged to Zora "Zo" Tucker from Hartford, Connecticut. Zora was the only white girl Boon had dated exclusively, but she looked like Carmen Electra, and everybody wanted her. She had full lips and big, perky breasts. The crazy part was that she had a black girl's ass. She and Boon spent a great deal of time together, but Boon played basketball and spent a great deal of time away from Chicago. Zora and Boon were expecting a son to be born in August of 2010. Donovan and Drakus talked Boon into getting a DNA test on the baby boy, because they truthfully didn't like the idea of their brother being in a relationship with a white girl. When baby Daniel's DNA test proved Boon was not the father, he left the hospital, disgusted, and never saw Zo again.

Boon looked at *his son's* ultrasound picture and anger flooded his face.

Next up, was the bag he kept for the memories of "Gia"; Ms. Giovanni Frazier. Gia was from Raleigh, North Carolina. He met her at a frat party, during his freshman year at DePaul. His roommate's girlfriend and Gia were room-mates. She was timid and not used to being away from home. She liked Boon and his sense of humor. Boon liked her body, her tattoos, and that she would go all the way when you closed the door. She often went back to visit her family in North Carolina; and during one of those visits, she was on the phone with Boon when her ex-boyfriend, Shyne, came over.

"Boon, I'ma call you back in a minute," she said, but somehow didn't hang up the phone. Boon stayed on the line and heard the whole, 24-minute, sex session they had. By the time she got back, Boon had sexed two of her sorority sisters and Gia transferred to UNC-Asheville the next semester.

Ebony "Lil" Charles was the smallest of Boon's exes. She was only 4'11, but was stacked. Big ass, big titties, and she could dance like no other. She was from Cabrini Green, just Northwest of Downtown Chicago. Boon rushed into the relationship with Lil, because the girlfriend he'd left wouldn't have sex. Lil definitely put out; in fact, it was the reason Boon left her. He caught her at a party, getting a train run on her by at least six of the players on Simeon's football team. Boon was the laughingstock of his senior class.

That brought him to the last bag, reserved for "CiCi", Boon's favorite girl. Boon had tried to be her boyfriend since 7th grade and she had turned him down until 10th grade. In 10th and 11th grade, they were voted as Simeon High School's "cutest couple". They were prom King and Queen their junior year, and they both were scholars.

Curelle was 5'7 and weighed about 170 pounds. She was dark-skinned and thick. All the guys were jealous of Boon because they wanted CiCi. She told Boon he would be her first, but not until graduation day. Boon didn't make it; he broke her heart by breaking up with her to be with Lil, all because Lil would sex him when he wanted it. He and CiCi were still great friends, but she said she couldn't trust him with her love anymore. "And now, every bitch I want, want every nigga but me," Boon said aloud. *Bunch of harlots*.

Relocated

6 Months later

Boon graduated law school and passed the bar with flying colors. It was the beginning of the summer and Boon had been doing well. He was doing a little dating, but nothing too serious. He had moved to a brand-new loft in South Loop. After careful consideration, he felt it was best. Johan kept blowing up his phone and Boon really wanted to put the beaters on him. When Boon packed, as he was preparing to move, he found that Mela stole his *stash* of cash he kept in his closet: $9000 that he kept in an old, Stacy Adams shoebox. He didn't even bother to pursue the issue. "Good riddance to bad rubbish," he said, as he unpacked in his new abode.

Boon was out on a mission, after growing tired of unpacking his belongings. He had a date tonight with a girl named Shardae, whom he had met at a deli the same week he found his new home. Shardae and Boon had both wanted the last slice of key lime pie the deli had. Boon ordered it first, so by rule of the restaurant, it was his.

"I mean, if you're willing to let me take you on a date, you can have the pie and I'll even pay for it," Boon had told her. Almost as soon as he told her that, he realized it was a mawkish comment, but it was too late to take it back. Much to Boon's surprise and liking, Shardae accepted.

"I'm glad you didn't come at me with the disrespectful stuff. That corny move just got you a date," Shardae gushed, as she exchanged numbers with him.

Boon was a little embarrassed, when she called his pickup line corny; but hell, he thought it was too. Shardae was almost a Stacy Dash look-a-like, but with more hips, bust, and ass. She was no taller than 5'4 and wore her hair in some honey blonde micro braids.

Boon was looking for an outfit to wear tonight; he and Shardae were going to the Cubs game. "Shar", as she went by, had never been to a professional sporting event and eagerly wanted to go. As he walked in Footlocker, he heard a female voice call his name from behind.

"Daniel Watson? It can't be!" the woman said.

Boon froze in his tracks and turned to see whom it was that had called his name. It was none other than Taz. Boon frowned, as soon as he recognized her. She was gorgeous in her grey, Hermès, summer dress with the sandals and handbag to match. Just seeing her caused

Boon's loins to go crazy; however, he felt some type of way about how she had left him. *Gold digger*.

"Tatiyana Lopes," he said, dryly. "Surprised you know who the hell I am," Boon stated.

"Well, aren't we bitter?" Taz poked fun at him. "The dick was great, Boon, you just couldn't afford a bitch like me. I'm a few levels above your pay grade, or have you gotten yo' cash right?" Taz retorted.

"Bitch, fuck you. Apparently, yo' scandalous-ass ain't got yo' mind right yet," Boon snapped and walked into the shoe store.

It had been months since a broad had remotely pissed Boon off, and the last time had almost proved fatal. He sometimes woke from dreams of killing Mela for fucking his *supposed-to-be* homeboy.

"Can I help you find something, sir?" the teenaged salesperson asked Boon.

"Yeah, if you can tell me what kinda drugs these hoes on that got them actin' all cocky." Boon was still a little miffed. The salesman only shrugged his shoulders. "Gimme these and these in a size ten and a half, li'l bruh," Boon said, referring to the same pair of Kevin Durant's in different color schemes.

It was about 2:00 p.m. and Boon wasn't set to meet Shardae until 7:00. Boon got into his Challenger, fired up his engine, turned on Pandora Radio from his phone, and pulled off. Before he was even five minutes removed from the mall, his music was interrupted by his phone's incoming call. His phone was connected to his radio, so he could hear his conversation through his speakers. He didn't recognize the number, but he answered anyway.

"Wazzup?" he said to the caller.

"Can I talk to Boon?" a woman's voice asked.

"Who this?" Boon asked, as he made a right turn, half a mile away from his destination.

"This is...wait, promise me you won't hang up first."

"Man, hell naw. I ain't promisin' shit. Who are you?"

"Please, Boon. Tell me you won't hang up once I tell you."

"Okay. I won't hang up. Now, who is this, actin' 17 and shit?" Boon asked, becoming annoyed.

The voice was sexy, coming through his speakers, but Taz had pissed him off already, so he was in a fucked up mood.

"This is Gia. Giovanni Frazier. You remem— "

Boon hung up. Rick Ross's "Hit You From The Back" was playing on Pandora. It was interrupted twice more, before Boon finally answered.

"What you want, Gia? Huh?" he yelled. "You died to me when you did that triflin' shit."

If the episode with Taz earlier hadn't pissed him off, this shit definitely did the trick.

"Boon… baby, I'm sorry. I— "

Boon hung up again. He wanted answers too; he just had to get her irritated first. After all, she fucked up, not him.

The next call from Gia went a bit more civilly. In the end, she convinced Boon to meet up with her after his date with Shardae. Boon said he didn't trust her enough to come to her, so he'd tell her where to meet him after he left Shardae.

Boon wondered if any other man went through the type of shit that he went through with women. Of course, they got dumped, but the shit Boon encountered had to be on another level.

"I should kill these hoes for playin' wit' pimpin'," he joked, as he dropped Shardae off after their date and pulled away. He'd had a good time at the game with her; he'd even scheduled a dinner date with her for later in the week. For whatever reason though, he could not get his mind off Gia. He thought about how sexy her ass sat in a pair of boy shorts. How she moaned his name when she rode him and let him dive deep into her love glove from behind. Most of all, he thought of when she had fucked Shyne and he had heard it all. For some strange reason, being pissed like that was giving him a rush. Combined with his encounter with Taz earlier, and the thoughts of Mela from months ago, this shit with Gia only intensified the rush, and Boon began to smile wickedly. He grabbed his phone to call Gia.

"I thought you was gon' stand me up, Daddy," Gia said, as Boon unlocked his car door and let her in at the Texaco.

"I was," he said, almost seriously.

Gia sucked her teeth. "Stop playing." She leaned over, kissed Boon on his ear and sat her purse on the backseat.

Boon couldn't be mad right now if he wanted to. Gia had on a yellow tennis skirt made by Ralph Lauren and a white Ralph Lauren T-shirt, with yellow sleeves. She smelled like something Boon wanted to lick off her. *She knew what she*

*was doing, dressing sexy and smelling all
provocatively and shit.*

"So, where to?" Boon asked, trying to
compose himself and tame his third leg.

"Let's find us a lounge or somethin'. I wanna
hear some music, but I still wanna talk to you,"
Gia said, rubbing Boon's thigh.

Boon reclined his head in understanding,
turned up the Yo Gotti song on the radio, and
worked his way through traffic.

After a short drive to the Westside, Boon
found the perfect spot. An upscale lounge/bar
called Three Sheets. The couple entered and
found a nice, cozy booth in the corner. A waiter
approached and asked if they were ready to
order.

"Let me get a 20-piece order of lemon pepper
wings, Grey Goose and orange juice, and a
Cosmo for the lady," Boon said.

He knew what Gia wanted; it was her
favorite drink.

"You remembered," she murmured, with a
look of remorse.

"Is that a bad thing that I did?" Boon asked,
when he saw her expression.

"No. I just...I...wanna make shit okay
between us, Boon," she said, looking solemn. "I
fucked up and I know this, but I miss the hell out

29

of you," Gia whimpered, with glossy eyes, as though she might cry.

"Yeah, well, yesterday is forever the same, but today and tomorrow can be altered. So, which will you focus on?" Boon asked, wiping a falling tear from his ex-lover's face.

"Damn, you still got a way with those words, boy," Gia said, as the waiter brought out their drinks and sat them in front of them.

"Wings'll be out in just a minute," the waiter said, as Boon handed him $40 and declined the change.

"Can I ask you a question?" Gia asked, as she took a couple sips from her Cosmopolitan. Boon nodded. "Do you still love me?" she asked.

Boon looked her in the eyes and told her, "Real love never dies. I just don't trust you, playa."

"I deserved that." Gia nodded.

The waiter appeared with the wings and Boon ordered another round of the same drinks. The liquor was doing its job, as both Boon and Gia caught up on old times. Gia answered a few text messages, but, otherwise, gave Boon her undivided attention all night.

"You 'bout ready?" Gia asked Boon, when he sat his glass down.

"Yeah, I ain't drunk, but I will be if I have another one," he said, standing up and following Gia out of the lounge.

He could not take his eyes off her ass, the entire walk to the car.

"Can I go home with you tonight, Boon?" she asked, bluntly.

"I don't care, G. At least I ain't got to do much driving," Boon said, pulling into traffic.

"Oh, actually, I was hoping you would be in the mood for a li'l ride when I got you home, Daddy." Gia rubbed Boon's chest and stomach.

Boon mashed the gas a bit harder.

*

"I just moved in here yesterday, so excuse all my shit every—"

They had barely made it into the apartment before Gia was on him, kissing him and with her legs wrapped firmly around his waist. He gripped her ass cheeks and they kissed passionately. He could feel the warmth from her juice box on the zipper of his Robin's shorts. She jumped down and unbuckled his belt, as he gently squeezed both her breasts, before pulling off her shirt. She got his shorts down and pulled his elongated manhood through the hole in his

31

boxers. She kissed the head of it, letting Boon feel her MAC lip gloss, while he pulled up her skirt and palmed both her thick, but soft, ass cheeks. Just as he slapped her bottom, she slid his length into her mouth.

"Mmmm..." she moaned, as she slowly bobbed up and down on Boon's pleasure pole.

"Damn, Gia! I miss this mouth, girl," Boon groaned, throwing his head back, as he slowly fucked her mouth. Gia slurped him faster and moaned even louder. She eased Boon to the floor, still simultaneously jacking and sucking his pipe, and slipped off her soaked G-string. Boon reached for his shorts and got a condom out of the pocket. Gia took it and used her mouth to put it on, rubbing her throbbing clit all the while. She stood and then hovered over Boon's hardened rod, before easing him inside of her.

"Damn, this dick's bigger than I remembered," Gia said, riding slowly, to get reacquainted with a dick that had pleasured her years ago, on several occasions.

"Take that dick, Gia!" All of it!" Boon demanded, raising his hips to give her all the wood, as she came down.

"Oh fuck, Boon. Ohh…fuck me!" Gia exclaimed, as she bounced. Boon kissed her nipples, as her size 36D breasts bounced in the same rhythm.

"Turn yo' sexy-ass around." Boon wanted to watch her ride backwards. As Gia got up to reverse cowgirl, her phone rang. The ringtone was Beyoncé's "Drunk in Love".

"Baby, I'm sorry, but I gotta get that." Gia crawled to her Chanel purse.

"The fuck?" Boon sat up, wondering if this bitch was serious. Gia was on her hands and knees, scrolling through her phone, after missing the message. Boon eased up behind her, on his knees, and gripped her hips, as he entered her.

"Wait… ooh… baby." Gia put her face on the floor and let Boon work her over with his magic stick.

Boon, looking down, saw *Shyne* tatted on her right ass cheek, as he spread them apart and it reignited his fury. He began to pound Gia out with no remorse, causing her to moan louder, until they both climaxed.

Within minutes of the session, Gia was hibernating. Boon, still peeved, lay on the sofa bed next to her, wide awake. *This triflin' bitch in my life again*, Boon thought, as he stared at the ceiling.

Bzzzz.

Her phone vibrated against the floor. Under normal circumstances, Boon wouldn't have touched it, but he wanted to see who it was. When he got to the phone, it no longer buzzed; but much to Boon's surprise, it wasn't locked. He looked back to make sure Gia was still asleep. *Tore yo' ass up*, Boon smirked, as he saw that she hadn't even changed positions. He turned back to the phone and went to her text messages.

U betta not have sucked dat nigga up, read the first message Boon came to.

Boon frowned and looked at the contact the message was from. Someone named *"My Luv"* sent the message. Boon shook his head, exhaled slowly, and went to the message before that.

My Luv: Make sho' u make that lame put on a rubber!

Boon got pissed and began reading all 15 messages "My Luv" had sent since Gia called him earlier. One in particular stood out:

My Luv: Try to hit him up for at least 20 thou. U kno that fuck nigga love u.

Boon was ready to wake this scandalous bitch up and put her out. However, he had thought about his get-back and didn't want to alert her. It was hard to sleep before, but it

34

would be impossible now. Revenge is best
served cold, and Boon's heart was turning arctic.

Homecoming

"Girl, you better get dressed; the game is in an hour and I still gotta drop Pooh off with my mama." Sherie snaked her neck, as she put on her new earrings. "You all in that yearbook and shit. That nigga ain't comin'," she taunted her.

"Maybe he misses me too though," said Zora, upset with life after Boon. "I'm just being optimistic. He did love me." Zora got up and put on her grey, form-fitting, Fendi dress, with Fendi written in navy blue and her indigo Fendi heels. "What nigga ain't gon' want summa this?" she asked, rhetorically, looking at her back shot in the full-length mirror.

"Zo, come on, chick. We runnin' late already."

***

Boon decided to let Gia leave without incident or alerting her to his knowledge of the text messages. He declined to give her money, simply stating that being brokenhearted so many times over the years had made him guarded. She told him that she was in some legal trouble, and asked for 10 grand instead. Gia begged continuously and he told her he would think about it. She left without a fight, but told him she'd call him after the homecoming game.

Boon wanted to show DePaul what he had become tonight. He was major, on the legal defense scene, and well sought after. He donned a pair of white Polo slacks, white, long-sleeved, Polo button-down, powder blue sweater vest, white, furry Kangol, and fresh, white Air Force One's. He carried his AmEx Black Card and $2500 in cash, just in case. Boon sprayed a little Creed cologne on himself and walked out the door, got in his car and started the engine.

"DePaul, Daddy's comin' to homecomin'," he said, as he turned up the "Fuck You" song by Yo Gotti and Meek Mill.

*

"So we meet again, Boon. You gon' chump me off again?" Taz walked towards Boon, looking like a contestant on *America's Next Top Model*.

"I felt disrespected. I shot back," Boon said, defensively, as he and Taz handed their tickets to the men at the booth.

"I don't want no trouble, Boon. You lookin' good enough to go through, I must say." Taz looked him up and down.

Boon was surprised, but he liked it. Taz was a welcomed sight, with her long, auburn hair and hazel eyes. The white and black Prada gauchos she wore made it look as if she had two asses.

"Thanks, Taz. You could get it too." Boon flirted, as they walked towards the entrance.

"I might just take you up on that." Taz winked and went toward the concession stand. Before she walked away, she turned and said, "Lemme get that number. I think I do wanna put you on the menu."

Boon couldn't resist. How could he? He would give Taz children, if she let him. They exchanged numbers and parted ways. Boon was having a decent day, so far, and wondered who else he might run into before the night ended. He found his seat three rows from half-court, just as the ticket holders of the three seats to Boon's left came to claim them.

"Goose. Goose?" Boon called.

"Daniel Boon. What's up, boy?" the man greeted. "Man, ain't seen you since sophomore year. You been a'ight though, I hear," Goose said.

He was black as night and weirdly skinny, with a long neck; hence the name *Goose*.

"I try to make shit happen, boss," Boon said, modestly.

"Oh, guess who I saw on the way in here though?" Goose asked, widening his eyes, making himself look like Daffy Duck with his beak missing.

"Who?" Boon asked, curiously.

"Ol' dirty-ass Zo. She wit' her cousin, Sherie. You know, the one from Peoria."

Boon's heart fluttered and he looked as though he was hurt.

"Excuse me. I gotta whizz before the game jump off," he said, as he got up and walked away from his seat.

"Somethin' ain't right," Boon said to himself, as he splashed water on his face in the bathroom. "I know it's homecomin' weekend, but the three women I fell for are all here. Right now," he thought aloud. He instantly thought of the doctor giving him the DNA results, proving he hadn't fathered Zo's baby. He quickly became infuriated. His brothers had teased him at several of the family functions that followed. *I'm not staying at the game.* Boon left the bathroom and headed to a local sports bar to watch the game. He was going to the frat and homecoming after-party when the game was over, so he wasn't ready to go home yet.

The game was now over and it was party time. Boon called up Drakus and Damian, who were both supposed to meet him at the party. Drakus was married and had been for four years now. Damian was recently divorced and loving it. They were already at the party, awaiting Boon's arrival. Before Boon could even get in his parking space good, Meek Mill alerted him of an incoming text message. It was from Taz.

Taz: Lemme b yo after party.

Boon grinned and texted back.

Boon: We'll see.

Boon got out of his car and went to meet his brothers inside the frat house.

Once inside, the first thing Boon noticed was the effect the black light had on the party. Everybody and everything looked almost purple. The women's shapes were even more profound. The music was blaring and you could see kegs and beer bottles everywhere. Boon walked towards the kitchen to find Drakus.

"What up, li'l bruh?" Drakus yelled over the music.

"Shit, man…runnin' from the hoes of relationships past and shit." Boon and Drakus both laughed. "Where Dooly at?" Boon asked, referring to Damian.

"He just walked off wit' some skirt he just caught up wit'," Drakus said. "Oh, yeah," Drakus continued, as he sat his beer down and leaned in to speak in Boon's ear, "Zo is on the hunt for you, boy. She done came to me twice to see if you was here. I'm just sayin'." Drakus stepped back and winked.

Just as he began to reply, he was tapped on the shoulder, only to turn around and discover Zora Tucker standing before him.

"Hello, Boon," she said.

Boon couldn't hear her, but he knew what she said. He only nodded, as if to say, "What's up?"

Zo mouthed something else, but Boon couldn't hear what it was. He leaned over, so she could say it in his ear.

"Mind if we talk for a moment or two on the lawn?" she repeated.

Boon extended his arm, palm open, facing the ceiling, motioning for Zo to lead the way. Boon looked back at Drakus, who was shaking his head at his baby brother.

"I miss being here. The parties. The scenery. Do you miss college, Boon?" Zo started.

"Pretty fucked up way to open up, Zo!" Boon wasn't about to be toyed with. Zo seemed surprised by his response.

"Well, damn. My bad," Zora apologized. "How you like my dress?" She quickly changed the subject.

"How yo' baby daddy like yo' dress?" Boon retorted.

41

His brothers had tormented him for years, and it was on full display in his tone. Zo only hung her head.

"Boon, I can't apologize enough for that. For the last six years, I have beaten myself up for what I did." A single tear rolled down Zo's cheek. "Boon, he even looks like you," she continued.

This made Boon swell with anger.

"But he ain't mine, Zo! You gave that twat up on me, unprotected. What, man…what you lookin' for me for? Real shit," Boon asked, impatiently.

Zo paused to wipe her tears and gather her thoughts. "Honestly, I was hoping we could talk about us. Maybe we could try again. Be a family." Zo said, searching Boon's face for his feelings.

"Are you fucking serious right now?" he asked. "You pull a fuckin' Maury Povich on me, got the whole city of Chicago lookin' at me like the whipping boy, and you got the nerve to ask me about *us*?" Boon was livid. "Yo' *us* is wit' yo' kid's daddy, Zo. And I'd appreciate it if you'd change the li'l nigga name from Daniel too!" Boon turned around, heading back into the party.

Zo called his name several times from behind him, but he ignored her.

"How'd it go, kid?" Drakus asked Boon, as he sensed the frustration emanating from his youngest sibling.

"Fuck is wrong wit' broads?" Boon asked, rhetorically.

"Them just yo' broads, bruh," Drakus slurred, obviously feeling his liquor. "It's a trillion fish out there, Boon. You just keep stickin' yo' dick in the wrong damn pond." Both men laughed at this, but Boon still felt some type of way.

Boon and Drakus saw Damian walking towards them with three women. They appeared to be triplets.

"This is Ashley, Alexis, and Amerie. They're triplets," Damian said. The women looked Hawaiian and were identical to one another, including their shapes. "I told them it was ironic, because there were two niggas downstairs who looked like me too." The group laughed, as Boon and Drakus introduced themselves. Boon quickly leaned in to whisper in Amerie's ear, and she led him to the dance floor. He was surprised to hear the young lady talk. She was from San Bernardino, California and had graduated from DePaul last year.

"I'm studying a lawyer," she told Boon.

"Funny…me too. Must be fate," Boon replied.

After multiple dances and the most incredible conversation, Boon and Amerie exchanged numbers and vowed to get to know each other better. Soon, the party was dying down and Boon was ready to go.

"Bruh, drop me off. I'm too drunk to drive and yo' sister-in-law gon' kill me if I don't go home," Drakus said, as he climbed off the couch and followed Boon to his car.

As Boon got to his car and cranked it, his phone rang.

"What up?" he answered.

"You ready for me?" Taz asked.

Boon was anxious. "Hell yeah, but you gotta come to me though," Boon said.

"I'm not drivin' though, baby," Taz whined.

"Get one of your homegirls to bring you, or a cab or somethin'. I'll pay. My brother a li'l inebriated and I gotta drop him off," Boon said, pulling off and listening to Drakus snoring in the passenger seat.

Taz agreed and Boon gave her the address. He dropped Drakus off and headed home. On his way home, Boon's phone rang again. He looked at the screen and saw his sister, Deysha, smiling at him.

"Mae, what you doing up so late, girl?" Boon called his older and favorite sister by her childhood nickname. Her middle name was Tremè, but the family called her Mae for short.

"Just checkin' on my baby brother. I done called Dooly and Drake already. I know y'all was goin' to the party tonight," she said.

Deysha was exactly 5 foot tall, 130 pounds, and dark-skinned with long, pretty hair. She was very loving to those she loved, but Mae was also a firecracker.

"Fa'sho. I'm good. On my way home to get ready for Taz… " Boon abruptly stopped speaking. He remembered that Mae had beat Taz up for talking recklessly to and about Boon some years ago. Boon knew Mae was about to go off.

"The hell you getting ready to do with her?" she asked, putting her full attitude on display.

"I'm not finna do shit," Boon lied.

"Boy, you ain't gon' learn. Leave them no-business-havin', broke-ass hoes alone. You got too much goin' on fa yo'self. Yo' dick don't attract nothin' but triflin'-ass women, bruh," she hollered.

"Damn," Boon muttered.

"Damn is right. You're grown though, so just be careful, baby brother. And tell that ho I said walk light," Mae responded. She and Boon said their good-nights, and hung up the phone.

Boon got in the house and kicked out of his Nike's. He texted Taz and told her to be on her way. It was almost 3:00 a.m., and for some odd reason, Boon thought about CiCi. He sent her a text to see if she was awake. She didn't have a significant other at the moment, and would usually call or text back if she was awake.

Boon went to the bathroom to take a leak. "Damn beer is runnin' through me," he groaned aloud, as he relieved himself. After flushing the toilet and washing his hands, he heard the phone ring. He ran and grabbed it, expecting Taz to be on the other end; it was CiCi, however, and Boon happily answered.

"Wassup, wifey?" he greeted her, as he always did.

"Probably one of yo' li'l skank's legs over there," she retorted.

"Funny. Man, why I run into Zo, Taz, and Gia in the same week? And they all act like we never had a fucked up spot in our history at all. All three of them!" Boon exclaimed.

"You and yo' li'l bird gang. Did you keep yo' cool? Or did you lose it?" CiCi asked. She was very attentive and actually cared about what went on in Boon's life. She truly would be with him, if only he would slow down and court her again.

"I lost it on all three of them hoes; especially, Gia. This ho had the nerve to ask me for some money!" Boon recalled.

"I told you them bitches ain't shit," CiCi said. Boon laughed at the fact that it was Mela's ringtone in his phone. Boon parted his lips to speak again, but there was a knock at the door.

"CiCi, lemme go do number six and I'ma call you back." Boon lied, because he didn't want CiCi to know that Taz was coming, and he was sure that's who had knocked.

"I'm 'bout to crash, baby… I mean... Boon; just call me tomorrow."

CiCi had called him baby, and he heard it loud and clear. He would have to talk to her in depth on that… but, at another time. "Okay then," he said and hung up.

"Well, don't you look edible," Boon flirted with Taz. She had changed clothes and was now wearing a leopard print catsuit with matching heels. Boon was sexing her with his eyes, as she posed in the doorway.

"Ain't you gon' let me in?" Taz asked. Boon didn't respond, he just stepped aside and watched her strut past him.

"You thirsty?" he asked, as he closed and locked the door.

"I came to get stroked, Mister Watson. So, are you gonna stab me or not?" Taz was standing with her hands on her hips in a model-like stance, piercing him with her provocative eyes.

"Lemme go take a leak, and then we can do the damn thang," Boon anxiously uttered on his way to the bathroom.

For the next two hours, Taz took Boon to ecstasy in ways he couldn't recall from their prior sexual endeavors. Although Taz was moaning and yelling his name, Boon was the one feeling as if he was the one under a spell—straight whipped. The couple tasted and kissed each other, as if they were in love, and made that deep eye contact that you make with someone you don't ever want to let go. After multiple orgasms and a blunt of Kush, the couple lay sprawled out across the living room floor.

"Boon, can I tell you something?" Taz asked, as she sat up on her elbow.

"I'm all ears, Miss Lopes," Boon replied, staring at the ceiling.

"You know I never, ever, stopped loving you, right?"

It caught Boon off guard, because even when they were a couple, he'd only heard her tell him she loved him less than 10 times. Boon was lost in his thoughts, but didn't want her to feel like he didn't care himself.

"Is that right?" he asked, almost sounding serious.

Taz mushed him and said, "I'm for real, boy."

Boon was trapped; he didn't want to tell her the truth, which was that he loved her too. Hell, he loved every girlfriend he had ever had. Now, he had several "partners"; but the girlfriends, he actually gave them love.

"I love you too, you sexy ma'fucka, you," he said, stroking her chin, as she leaned in and gave him a long, deep kiss - tongue and all.

***

"Get yo' weak-ass up, nigga!" a man's voice boomed. Boon was knocked out sleeping, but slowly began to wake up. He thought he was dreaming, until he felt the sudden thump against his head and the agony that followed it directly after.

"Ah, fuck! Man, what the fuck is this?" he yelled, as he reached for the now-leaking side of his scalp.

"You know what the fuck this is. You sit here and shut the fuck up. We take what we want and we leave. Anything short of that, will have a story about your life ending on the news in a couple hours." The gunman's voice sounded menacing and deadly serious, as he hovered over Boon.

As Boon surveyed the room, he saw two other men flipping all of his belongings over. They had already taken down his flat screen. The glass dining room table had been shattered, as well as the abnormally large aquarium. Boon sat there, helplessly, as his fish flopped around on the wet carpet in broken glass and gravel, desperately searching for water. *I thought I had moved away from this kind of shit.* Boon grimaced at the pain and ringing in his ear.

One of the other two men in the house grabbed the remaining cash from the Polo slacks Boon had worn last night, and his jewelry off the table. He also grabbed Boon's cellphone and threw it in the kitchen sink, right before the faucet came on.

"See, every robbery don't have to involve killing somebody," the man hovering over Boon said. Boon still couldn't really make out much, because of the throbbing headache, but it seemed like he'd make it out of this one alive. The men headed towards the front door to make their exit; and just before the gunman walked out, he turned to Boon and said, "Yo, tell Taz— provided you see her again— that Krumb said, 'we even'." He touched his gun to his forehead lightly, in a salute, and walked out without closing the door behind him.

Brand New

"Ol' scandalous-ass bitch!" Boon yelled, after slamming the door and locking it behind him. He hadn't even realized it, until the masked gunman had brought it to his attention—Taz wasn't there. His first thought was to call the police, but Boon thought better of it.

"I can't report this shit. Snitchin' ain't in me and they get buried in Chi-Town," Boon thought aloud. He looked around his crib at the mess the robbers left. He felt himself getting angrier by the minute. So many different thoughts ran through his mind at once: retaliation, paying someone to whip Taz's ass, or maybe involving his brothers. He knew he couldn't involve his brothers, though; they were the ones who'd shared a hearty laugh when Boon found out that Zo's baby wasn't his. Boon was so furious that smoke was nearly visible coming from his ears.

"Fuck everybody!" he yelled in a rage. He went to his bedroom and found his car keys, which were lying on the floor in front of his bedroom window. Before picking them up, he stopped in front of the mirror on his dresser to assess the wound on the side of his head. The bleeding had stopped and the gash was barely visible, due to the dried blood around it. Boon was thankful to have left his wallet in the glove compartment of his car.

The sun was slowly rising and peeking through the blinds, as Boon was getting dressed in jogging pants and a T-shirt. He was going to the hospital to get sewn up, and then he would go get a new phone. His mind was on his choice of women in his past. None of them turned out to be good for him, not one— except for CiCi. However, CiCi wouldn't take him back now. She knew too much about him and his *"skanches,"* as she referred to Boon's lovers. Boon shook his head to clear it and tried to figure out who to call to keep him company at the ER.

He went into the kitchen and fished his phone out of the sink. Although it was only partially submerged in the water, it was clearly on the fritz. Miraculously, he was able to view the first two contacts in the phone, and he quickly wrote the numbers down. Amerie, whom he had met the night before, was the first one. Ariel, his sister-in-law and Drakus' wife, was the second. "Hell no," he muttered, at the thought of calling his brother's wife; she'd just tell Drakus and he'd alert the entire family. *Fuck it, I'ma call CiCi when I get there.* He put the wet phone in a Ziploc bag and headed out the door.

After making sure he got to his car safely, Boon drove to a nearby gas station to use a payphone. He called CiCi three different times and got the voicemail with each attempt. "Dammit!" he yelled, as he slammed the phone back on the hook, without leaving a message. He then dialed Amerie's number, and much to his surprise, not only did she answer, she sounded wide-awake.

"Hello?" she said in a tone that seemed to wonder who the hell would be calling her at 6:15 a.m.

"Sorry to call so early. C-can I speak to Amerie?" Boon stammered, nervously.

"This is Amerie; who's calling?" she asked, with the curiosity still evident in her tone.

"It's Boon, the gentleman you met at the frat party last night."

"Oh! The cutie in the Polo. You don't waste time, huh?" she teased.

"I would've waited, but I kinda got a li'l situation I need some help wit' right now."

"Like what? Ain't givin' you no money, boy," Amerie said solemnly.

Boon chuckled. "I got plenty money, baby. That's the problem though. I got robbed last night and was hit with a pistol. I know this will be a crazy first date, but can you come sit wit' me while I get stitched up?" Boon asked, pouting, as if she could see him.

"Oh my God! Are you okay?"

"I will be, with you there, and some pain medication."

"Sure, I'll come. I was only taking my morning jog. What hospital do I meet you at?" Amerie asked.

"Cook County," Boon told her, and she said she'd be there in 20 minutes, at the most.

By the time he saw Amerie walk into the waiting room, Boon had just signed in. Her tan skin was flawless and she looked perfect with no makeup on at all. She had her hair pulled back in a ponytail, and had on a green and yellow Nike jogging suit that hugged her frame. To complete the outfit, she was wearing matching, green and yellow Nike Huaraches on her feet. Boon's first thought was that she was an Oregon Ducks fan; his second thought was about how many ways he'd like to peel that jogging suit off and give her the dick.

"Over here, babe," Boon waved his hand in the air to let Amerie know where he was seated. It was also a ploy to let everyone in the waiting area know that she was there for him.

"How in the hell did this shit happen?" Amerie asked, once she was seated next to Boon.

"My dumbass had to take a leak bad as hell when I first got home. I ran in and didn't lock the door behind me. When I came back into the living room, three niggas was in my house with guns. One hit me, and I woke up like this," Boon lied. How could he tell her he was fucking his ex-girlfriend and fell asleep, only to wake up in the midst of the robbery, and find out that she was the one who had set the whole thing up?

"Damn, boo, at least you're alive." Amerie was caring, and Boon began to feel that tingle in his heart, all over again. "What made you call me? I'm sure you called your family after you called the cops."

"You were the first person I thought of when I regained consciousness," Boon lied, again. "My family would exaggerate the situation; mainly, because I'm the youngest."

"And the cops?" Amerie asked, as she put her hand on Boon's thigh.

"I'm from Chicago; we don't call 911. Besides, I'm alive and they only got some jewelry and some chump change," Boon smirked.

"All right, macho. So what— " Amerie was interrupted by the loudspeaker calling out a few names.

"I need a Jamela Howard and a Daniel Watson. Please, report to the nurse's station."

Boon's ears perked up like an alerted canine. Instead of instantly standing, Boon looked around to be certain he'd heard correctly. Just as sure as shit stinks, Mela was walking toward the doctor. She was obviously pregnant, and to top that off, she was with Yo.

"Daniel Watson, last call," the voice on the loudspeaker blared again.

"Boon, let's go. He's called your name three times now." Amerie was tugging at his arm for him to get up. By now, Mela was looking around suspiciously, waiting to see the man who would respond to that particular name. Reluctantly, Boon got up and walked with Amerie to where the doctor was standing.

As they walked up, Mela spoke first. "Damn, Boon! The fuck happened to you?" she asked. She actually seemed concerned, but Boon didn't even acknowledge her.

"Dag, homie, that's a big-ass gash, fam!" Yo exclaimed.

Boon's jaw gave away the fact that he was clenching his teeth, although he said nothing.

Both couples followed the doctor to the back towards the triage rooms.

"Uh-um…" Amerie cleared her throat, as if to get Boon's attention, but he ignored her because he was beyond pissed.

"Mister Watson, you'll take room three right here," the doctor pointed to his left and stuck the chart in the tray on the door.

"It's like that?" Mela scoffed. "Fuck you and ya li'l Barbie doll too, nigga!" Mela snarled, as she walked off with the doctor.

Boon smirked; it was all he could do to keep from spazzing out in the room. Inside, he was a fireball; an intense rage was building in him and he felt his eyes get watery. He was mad enough to kill at that very moment. *I shoulda choked the life outta that bitch.*

"Ummm, Boon?" Amerie broke into his thoughts of murderous rage. "Are you okay? I just called your name six times," she stated, as Boon sat in a chair by the door, fighting his anger.

"I apologize, beautiful. Just got lost in a serious thought for a minute there," he replied.

"So I noticed." Amerie sat down right next to Boon. "You wanna tell me who your friends were just a minute ago, or do I wait until you're stitched up and healed?" she asked, as he looked into her mesmerizing eyes. She had gorgeous eyes; the kind that seemed to be able to see right through you. It almost made it impossible to lie to her. And at that moment, Boon wasn't even considering doing so.

"The girl was my ex-girlfriend, Mela. The guy *was* my good friend, Johan, or Yo, as we called him." Boon took a deep breath and exhaled.

Amerie waited a few minutes, and then urged him on. "Oh come out with it already. There has to be more to the story," she stated. "You didn't speak when either one of them spoke to you. Then the bitch went all hostile, like I wouldn't drop kick her ratchet-ass or something," Amerie huffed, with an attitude.

Boon smiled on the inside. "Okay, okay," he began, taking another deep breath and exhaling before continuing. "I thought shit was going smooth with us. One day, I bought her favorite wine, massage oils, and all that good shit. I was gonna help her relax after a hard day's work, ya know? She gets in and drops the 'I don't wanna be with you. Maybe another girl will love you how you wanna be loved', bomb on me. Needless to say, I'm crushed." Boon's eyes dimmed, as he recalled that dreadful night, while Amerie hung on to every word. "Yo was my weed man at the time, aside from being my homie. Earlier that day, he'd told me to stop by and pick some up. 'Even if my door is closed, just come in', he told me. After Mela hit me with the fucked-up news, of course, I needed some bud." Boon looked at the floor and paused. "I walked in Yo's spot, 'cause his music was blaring, as usual. He couldn't hear me calling his name, so I walked back to his room; he had Mela bent over his dresser, screwing her brains out." Boon stopped.

"Nann one of them ain't shit, then," Amerie concluded. "She gon' cross him up too. That probably ain't even his baby," she snorted. "Just so you know, I ain't that type of girl. That's some thirsty shit right there."

Before and after receiving his stitches, Amerie listened, as Boon regaled her with tales about his fumbled attempts at love. "You ain't got no little dick, do you?" she blatantly asked him.

"Hell no," he laughed, thinking about how serious women are about not getting *pencil dick* for a mate.

As they were walking to Amerie's car in the visitor's parking lot, they realized that they had only been in the ER for a couple hours. "What

60

now?" she murmured, while unlocking the doors on her metallic grey Chevy Camaro.

Boon smiled, impressed with this woman's choice of transportation. "Well, I need a new phone, so I'm gonna go grab one; and I was hopin' to treat you to breakfast, seein' as how you were kind enough to come sit with me this morning," Boon offered.

"Ain't gon' lie, I am kinda hungry. Am I driving or are you?" Amerie quipped.

"I don't like leaving my car, so I'd rather just follow you," Boon suggested.

"So, where are we goin'?" Amerie started her car, as she waited for Boon's reply.

"First, we go to the Sprint store; then after that, breakfast. If you bougie, we can go upscale, but if you down-to-earth, we can hit IHOP." Boon searched Amerie's face to see if she was either.

"Oh shit, I love pancakes. Go get your car and come on."

She trailed Boon to the Sprint store first, and sat in her car waiting, while he went in to purchase a replacement phone. Once he got in his car, they drove down the street and pulled into IHOP's parking lot, parking side by side.

The couple was immediately seated, and ordered coffee, while they perused the menus.

Once they'd placed their orders, they sipped their coffee and sat in silence, taking in the scenery. It had only been a few hours since the last woman's presence he'd been in had added insult to injury. Quite naturally, Taz setting him up made him apprehensive with Amerie, no matter how much she smiled and seemed safe. After what seemed like an everlasting, awkward silence, Amerie cleared her throat and locked eyes with Boon when he turned to face her.

"Are you okay?" she asked.

"Honestly, nah," replied Boon, who was twiddling his thumbs and staring into those truth-serum-causing orbs that Amerie called eyes. "I just can't seem to find the right chick. I think it's because of me rushing things. I stay single for months, only to get into another dead-end situation. It could be because I go for a certain type of girl. I look for opposites, but no formula I try seems to work for me." Boon turned away from the eye contact, feeling awkward. *Why am I explaining this to her?*

Almost as if she heard his thoughts, Amerie said, "I'm glad you are honest with me. You're not afraid of your feelings, and not many men share that characteristic." Amerie reached across the table and grabbed Boon's hand. "Women often talk about men not hittin' on shit or how they ain't good for anything. Well, I say for every type of man that exists, there is a woman who's just like him. I think we might be a good look for each other. You just need some time off the dating scene for a little while." She was about to continue, but the waitress approached the table with their food.

"May I refill your coffee?" she asked, after she'd sat the plates down on the table.

"Yes, please," they answered, simultaneously. They both remained quiet until the waitress left.

"Amerie, I would love to begin dating and getting to know you better, but I've got so much baggage and bullshit that I don't want nobody dealing with, including myself," Boon blurted, as he poured strawberry syrup on his pancakes.

"I can understand that, but if you never come out to play again, you'll be an old, dull-ass guy and hate yourself for it. I'd hate for you to miss out on what a girl like me can do for you." Amerie winked her eye at him.

Boon nodded his head, contemplating, as he took in what she'd said. He shoveled a few pieces of his pancake in his mouth and let out an appreciative, "Mmmm."

"As a matter-of-fact, breakfast is on me, and I say we take it in for the day. That way, we can get better acquainted and you can begin recuperating," Amerie murmured, as she ate a forkful of food herself.

Boon didn't want to be taken as a nigga who was green, but damn, how bad could it be? Amerie had her own money, car, and a great job. She was beautiful and she didn't like how the other women had treated him. He pondered her offer; and after swallowing his food, he asked, "What's your idea of getting better acquainted?", while he fixed his coffee to his liking.

Amerie mused thoughtfully for a second, and then spoke. "Make no mistake about it, babe, you are an attractive man—a very attractive man, I admit; but I'm not tryna lay you down just yet. Not that I'm assuming those were your thoughts. I'm just putting that out there," she assured him while she waited for a response.

"Understood. So, what did you have in mind?"

"Well, what about Netflix?"

Boon wasn't quite expecting that; he liked Netflix, but he hadn't watched it in a few months. "Sounds good."

"Well, then, it's settled. We can go back to my place, kick-back, chill, and start preparing a list of things you need to replace at your house.

Whaddya say?" Amerie suggested, sliding her plate away from her; she was stuffed.

Boon had been so wrapped up in his breakfast with Amerie that he'd forgotten his house was in shambles from the robbery. "Sounds good. You ready now?"

"Yeah, let's get the check and go. I even have a big case coming up that you may be able to help me with. That is, of course, if you don't mind?" she hinted.

"On one condition," Boon requested. Amerie raised her eyebrow, wanting to know his terms. "Lemme pay for this breakfast," Boon stated, as he motioned for the waitress to bring their check.

Amerie smiled and exhaled softly. "Fine, but I get to pick the first movie when we make it to the house." Boon nodded his head in agreement.

Boon followed Amerie to a luxury townhouse in North Chicago and pulled in the driveway behind her. It was a nice-looking, red, brick building that gave off a very welcomed feel. Her grass was neatly manicured and she had a two-seater, swinging chair on her front porch.

"Damn, you got old folk amenities on your porch and shit," Boon quipped and chuckled.

"You so silly, boy. I sit there and watch my nephews play in the yard when they come over here," she responded, chuckling herself. Amerie took her keys and shuffled through them to locate the one to the front door. Once she found it, she unlocked the door, put the code in on the security pad, and let Boon in. She turned on the lights and Boon was in awe. Not only was Amerie's pad laid out, she had every game system that ever came out. The color scheme of her living room was lavender and grey, and she had two, enormous sectionals that seemed to seat at least 12 people each. There was a staircase immediately to the left of the entrance and a long hall in front of it. Boon could tell it led to the dining room and the kitchen.

"Ummm... make yourself at home. I'm gonna go shower and change. I'll be right back down," she said.

"I kinda wanna shower too. Do you have a washer and dryer here?" Boon asked.

"Sure. I'll get you situated. Just walk towards the kitchen; there's a bathroom just before you reach it. Towels and washcloths are in there. I'll bring you some soap and throw your clothes in the wash for you," Amerie said.

The duo met back up in the living room, on the couch, to watch TV after getting cleaned up.

Boon was in a towel and a throwback Karl Malone basketball jersey that Amerie swore didn't belong to an ex-boyfriend or one-night stand. She explained that she'd gotten it from a raffle she won at her sister's school a few weeks back.

"Mmm… you lookin' good in that jersey and towel," Amerie murmured, flirting with Boon.

"Girl, you shot-out. I'm a li'l cold though, for real," he retorted, rubbing the goosebumps on his arms.

"Hang on a sec, then. I'll be right back." She got up and walked upstairs. Boon thought that perhaps she'd gone to cut on the heat, or grab him a sweatshirt, at least. She returned with a king-sized, Chicago Bears blanket. Instead of giving the blanket to Boon, she sat beside him and threw the cover over both of them. The erection that followed was inevitable. Amerie smelled like Juicy Couture and was scantily clad in a Winnie the Pooh nightgown and some booty shorts. She snuggled close to Boon, as she used the PlayStation 3 controller to browse the available titles on Netflix. Amerie leaned across Boon's lap to get comfortable in a lying position, and jerked upright, as quickly as she'd lain down.

She looked at the bulge in the towel wrapped around his waist and then into his eyes. "What's good with that?"

Boon flushed with embarrassment. He didn't know if she was asking because she wanted it, or if she was asking why it was standing up like that. He looked at his lap and then back at Amerie. "I am extremely attracted to you, but I promise you, I…um…I didn't tell him to turn up on you like that," he stammered.

"You ain't on trial, Boon," Amerie laughed, turning her attention back towards the TV. "Nice to know you workin' with some real wood, though." She clicked the controller to start the movie *Ong Bak*, which happened to be one of Boon's favorite movies.

After the movie was over, they watched *Ong Bak 2*, and three other movies. By this time, Boon's clothes had washed and dried. The couple was now online searching for deals on flat screen TV's to replace the one that he'd lost in the robbery.

"I really just want to start over. I mean, I just moved to my new spot, so it's not too late to find something else," Boon stated.

"What are you going to do until then?"

"Hell, I don't know. Probably, get a room for about a month or so at one of those extended stays with the stove and all the cookware; everything furnished. Just until I find another spot."

"I wouldn't have a problem with you crashing here. I mean, if you'd like." Amerie sounded more anxious than she had intended to.

Boon was caught off guard. "I wouldn't want to impose on your situation here, beautiful. Besides, I'd feel like I was rushing into you, especially knowing that I would love to become more than your friend."

Amerie turned to face Boon and made eye contact. "We share sentiments in that aspect, but I'm a grown woman. If I want you to move in, that's my choice; it's yours to agree or disagree." She stood from her computer chair. Boon was standing right in front of her, as she stepped closer to him. "If I say I'm cool with you being here, or I want you here with me, then that's what I mean." She looked down at Boon's towel-clad waist. When she looked up again, Boon leaned in and began to kiss her. She didn't back off. In fact, she leaned her head to the side and opened her mouth enough to allow room for a meeting of their tongues. Amerie felt her love getting moist and she stepped back. "Get dressed; we goin' to get your things. You should plan to be here for a while."

Boon grabbed her hand, as she began to turn away, and pulled her to him. He kissed her lightly on her forehead. "Thank you. I feel good here with you. I'm nervous as fuck, but it's a good nervous." He let her go and got dressed. He was feeling Amerie and she felt the same way about him. It was good to feel these feelings in slow motion. For no apparent reason, however, Boon's mind began to attack him with thoughts of CiCi. He shook his head, as if to rid his mind of his thoughts, walked to the door to meet Amerie, and the couple hopped in her Camaro.

Picture-Perfect

As Amerie parked her Camaro, she reached into her Dolce & Gabbana purse and pulled out a chrome, snub-nose .38 revolver, with an ivory handle. Boon was a little shocked, but turned on at the same time. His facial expression reflected his sentiment. Amerie looked at him and said, "What? My dad gave all his girls straps. Chicago just ain't a safe haven, ya know?"

Boon lifted his hands in surrender. "Ain't judging; you ain't on trial." They shared a laugh.

"Hey, neighbor?" a man who lived under Boon called out to him, as he and Amerie started to ascend the flight of stairs to his abode. Boon stopped to see what the man wanted. "There was a young woman knocking at your door for about half an hour. She left and came back, knocked for about another half an hour. She even sat right there for a while." The man was pointing at the stairs in front of his unit.

Where was this nosy dude the night I got attacked? Boon wondered. "What'd she look like, homie?" Boon asked him.

"Oh, she was a sexy—" the man paused and looked at Amerie, unsure how to continue the description.

71

"You can finish, we're just friends," Amerie assured the man.

"Well, she said her name was Taz and that you knew her. She said she needed to talk to you about an incident. She left you her number." The neighbor handed Boon a piece of paper.

"Hey, bruh, I 'preciate it." Boon took the paper and continued up the stairs. When he looked back, Amerie had her .38 aimed and a "ready for whatever" look on her face. The couple entered the loft, cautiously, but no one seemed to have been there since Boon left for the ER.

"Damn! They fucked ya shit up!" Amerie exclaimed, taking in the scene in the living room. She walked into Boon's bedroom and paused at the door. "So, this is where the magic happens, huh?" she asked, staring at the California king bed.

"Nah. The magic happens right here." Boon was now standing in front of Amerie with his hand on his crotch. She blew him a kiss, as he turned back to get his stash from under his bed. He reluctantly pulled out his footlocker with the memorabilia from relationships past in it.

"What's that?" she asked, when he sat both cases on the bed.

"Dumbass robbers missed the real money," he said, opening the case of money, which contained $10,000 in 50's and 20's.

"Wow! You keep that kinda cash at your house all the time?" she asked, with a *no wonder you got robbed* tone in her voice.

"Yes. As a matter-of-fact, I do. It's a *just in case* sorta thing. Never know what may go down," Boon answered.

"Is the other one the same?" she inquired, taking a seat next to Boon on the bed. He was still quiet as a mouse, but staring at the box as if it was going to move on its own. "Am I not supposed to know what that box contains or something? I can step out and give you a minute or two." Amerie was about to stand, until Boon broke his silence.

"These are all of the harlots of my past. The trifling-ass broads I told you about. Pictures and minuscule memoirs that were supposed to remind me of good things," he said, as he opened the case. Amerie was rather anxious to see what type of taste he had. He had poor judgment of character, but damn, at least let these hoes look like something. Boon handed her four pictures.

"Which one is this?" Amerie held up one of the photos for Boon to identify.

"That's the one I caught, well... heard, having sex with her ex when she was supposedly visiting her family in North Carolina," Boon explained.

"Oh, the one who came to try to seduce you into giving her all ya li'l stash?"

Boon had only said she tried to seduce him; he'd left out the part about the sex they'd had. "Yep, Ms. Giovanni "Gia" Frazier," Boon said, nonchalantly. On the inside, he felt his pissed-off meter crank a few notches, but he didn't let it show.

"She ain't fine, but if I was a nigga, I'd slap bellies with her," Amerie said plainly and Boon laughed his ass off. "What? I mean, real shit; she not a 10. She's like a good six, six and a half, tops." Amerie had to laugh herself after she said that.

"Damn, girl, you cold-blooded," Boon said, still chuckling.

As Amerie went to the next picture, she handed Boon Gia's photo and he tossed it in the trash. Amerie pretended not to notice. "And this would be?" she held up the second photo.

"That is Zora "Zo" Tucker. She rubs a very fucked up spot in a nigga's mind," Boon murmured, thinking back to those test results.

Amerie didn't make it any better when she said, "Oh, so this is Ms. You Are Not The Father?" Her impression of Maury Povich caught Boon off guard and he looked at her as if he would push her into the wall. Instead, all he did was nod his head.

"Now, she's prettier than Gia; much prettier, in fact." She handed him the photo and he reunited it with the other photo he'd tossed in the trash. "Who in the hell is this? Wait, lemme guess. Is this the one you called Lil?" Amerie smirked, as she looked at the photo in her hand.

"Yep, Ebony Charles' black ass," Boon replied.

"Now this bitch is ugly as a muthafucka, boy. Ewww... I can't believe your fine-ass screwed this. If she was to put on some white overalls, she could be a brown-skinned Oompa Loompa." She and Boon laughed until they were teary-eyed. Boon used to tell her that all the time. Now, looking back, she was a li'l gremlin, but you know how niggas are, and she did have a fat ass on her.

The next picture she came to, after throwing Ebony's picture away for Boon, made her pause. "Now *this* is a bad bitch. This is a 10. I would applaud you in public with a bitch this fine," Amerie murmured.

Boon was seething. "That ho is the worst. That's Tatiyana "Taz" Lopes, the reason you had to meet me at the fuckin' hospital," he said, through gritted teeth.

"I'm sorry, baby boy. The bitch is crazy, but she still looks good though. If it makes you feel any better, I'll beat the bitch up when I see her. How 'bout it?" Boon didn't respond; he was holding a fifth picture in his hand and his thoughts were lost in it. Amerie threw Taz's picture back in the lockbox and took the picture from Boon's grasp. "CiCi, huh?" she asked.

"Yep, my best friend." Boon remembered at that moment that he hadn't told CiCi what happened to him. He'd called her a few times, but hadn't gotten an answer; he didn't bother to call back since, and then it slipped his mind.

"She is beautiful, Boon. You let a good girl get away, boy, but at least y'all maintained a good friendship out of the ordeal." She handed Boon the picture. "Now, you've got me," she said.

Boon abruptly stood up. "Let's go. Fuck this whole spot, babe. I'ma take this cash and just get all new everything when I find my new crib."

Amerie felt some type of way about Boon not responding to her last comment, but she knew he was going through the motions, so she didn't push the issue. "So, are you going to call her?"

They were back in the Camaro and Boon asked, "Call who?"

"Taz; remember your neighbor said she'd been by your place and left a number for you to call her?" Amerie glanced at Boon, briefly, before backing out of the parking space and heading back to her place.

"I'm still debating on that one. I really wanna crush her larynx, but I should have known not to trust her, so I'm thinking I should just eat that one," Boon replied. He felt like a real sucker; he had worked so many cases where his client confided in him that they'd actually committed the crime and how they'd used beautiful women to set it up.

"I say call her. Get some closure from the whole situation. I got your back; really, I do. I hate to see the good guys getting screwed over," Amerie said, sincerely. Boon didn't respond. They rode the rest of the way with the radio on, not speaking.

Once inside Amerie's house, Boon broke the quiet. "I need to go see my brothers and my sister; are you gonna be here for a while?" Boon asked Amerie, as she went to make them a light lunch.

"I'm not sure, but I hadn't planned on leaving. I've gotta work tomorrow. I was hoping we were still, you know, getting acquainted," she called out from the kitchen, where she was making shrimp scampi for the two of them.

"Oh, I'm definitely down for that. It's just that I haven't seen Dooly and Drake since the party, and my sister hasn't seen me in weeks." Boon responded. "Hey, what are you cookin' in there? That shit smells scrumptious!" he said, walking toward the kitchen.

Amerie was in front of the stove, getting her chef on. "A little shrimp scampi. I assumed we were both hungry, and not just my greedy behind," she quipped, as she felt Boon walk up behind her. His manhood was pressed against her posterior, but she didn't budge. She was more attracted to Boon, physically, than she had been letting on, and was nearly ready to throw her good girl in the closet. Boon rubbed her shoulders, and then leaned over and kissed her lightly on her neck.

Amerie fought, unsuccessfully, to keep a throaty moan from passing through her lips. She turned and placed her hands-on Boon's chest. After pushing him back softly, she said, "I want you. I want you bad. I've never given in to any guy within a month, let alone a week." She kissed his lips. "Let's have this lunch, and you go see your family. Take my spare key and let yourself back in when you get back." She looked in a drawer to the right of the stove, took out the key, and handed it to Boon. After sharing another deeply passionate kiss, she looked in his eyes and commented, "If I can't fight this feeling much longer, Boon, ya sexy-ass will be good and gotten tonight. Believe that."

Boon smiled like a kid who'd just seen 50 gifts under the Christmas tree - all with his name on them. "Say no mo'," was all he said.

After an enjoyable lunch, Boon kissed Amerie and left. He decided his first stop would be to the mall or something to get some more threads. Although what he had on had been laundered, it was what he'd had on for the last two days. He was sitting at a red light when he reached into his pocket to get his phone. When he pulled it out, along with it came the picture of CiCi that he and Amerie had looked at earlier. "Man, lemme call my muthafuckin' potna." He hooked his phone up to his stereo system and dialed her number.

"Hello, stranger," CiCi said, when she picked up the phone.

Boon chuckled to himself. He loved hearing her voice. No matter what stressed him, agitated him, or pressed him, CiCi was always a smile on his face waiting to happen. "Man, I tried to call ya ass early the other morning. Twice, to be exact," Boon told her.

"From where? The only number in my phone was from a payphone. I was asleep, trying not to fuck up my new hairstyle," she shot right back.

"That was me calling. My dumbass dropped my phone in the tub when we got off the phone. Not only that, I split my head on the coffee table, after tripping over my shoe on some drunk shit," Boon lied. *How can I tell CiCi that I let yet another woman get me in another fucked up predicament?*

"What the hell? Are you okay? You need me to come see about you?" CiCi was genuinely concerned about Boon. He didn't know it, but in her eyes, he was the one she'd let get away.

"I mean, I'm good now. I'm 'bout to do a little shoppin', if you wanna come fuck with me for a little while," Boon offered.

"You gotta come get me. I let my ma use my car today, since I didn't have to work," CiCi told him.

"Get dressed, I'm on the way to pick you up."

"Okay, how long before you pull up?" CiCi inquired. She wanted to jump in the shower before he got there.

"I'm 'bout 20 minutes away," he replied.

"Cool, I'll be ready." She ended the call.

Once Boon pulled up to CiCi's spot, he sent a text to his sister.

Boon: Deysha r u going to be home in the next hour? Tryna come thru.

Then, he called CiCi to let her know he was outside. When CiCi walked out, Boon fought to keep his jaw from dropping. She was the epitome of "Damn, she sexy!" She had on a pink, Juicy Couture jogging suit, pink and white Nike Huaraches, and her hair was feathered and long. The jogging suit was form-fitting, showed plenty of nice curves and ample ass.

"What up, dude?" she asked, with her normal, cool demeanor, once she was in the car. "Lemme see your head, boy." He turned his head to let her look at the stitched-up gash on the left side of his head. As he looked at her cleavage, he noticed she had on the B&C charm and necklace he bought her for Valentine's Day when they were in the 11th grade.

"You lookin' good as a mug, Curelle." Boon broke his silence by complimenting her, as she examined his scar.

81

"And you look like shit. No wonder you tryna go shopping," CiCi said, as she sat back in her seat and put on her seatbelt. She was always brutally honest, but Boon had always liked that about her. She didn't sugarcoat shit.

"Wow!" he exclaimed, as her comment wounded him.

"You still my boo though and you know that shit. Don't start trippin'. Now, let's ride; I'm sure you done had a few adventures that you can catch me up on."

Boon pulled into traffic and began to tell her about Amerie. He neglected to tell her about the kisses they had shared, or even the fact that he was living with her, albeit temporarily because Taz had set him up. He told CiCi that she'd come to sit with him at the hospital while he was seen about and had cooked for him as well. CiCi was unusually quiet, as she listened to him. As he glanced over at her, he was uncertain if it was intentional, but she looked as if she was jealous. "Are you a'ight?" he asked, as he pulled up to an empty space in the mall parking lot.

"I can't lie, I am a li'l jelly that I wasn't there to comfort you that night. I wish I had caught that phone call," she said, sullenly.

He unfastened his seatbelt and switched the ignition so that only the radio was playing. He turned to his best friend/ex-girlfriend and asked, "You almost called me baby the other night when we were ending our call. What's really good wit' you?"

CiCi removed her seatbelt as well and turned to face him. "You will always have my heart, Daniel, but I know we can't be together. I demand things from a man that you aren't prepared to give." She searched his face for a clue of his feelings. "All ya li'l skanches and ya li'l incidents wit' them; I be ready to bust a ho's head open 'bout my Boon now," she said, more excitedly than she intended to. She looked down into her hands. "Boon, I would love to be yours, but a lot of shit would need to be altered. A lot!" she said, grabbing the key ring in the middle console of the car and showing it to him. Let's go get you some new gear before somebody we know sees you like that."

Boon hadn't looked at the key ring before now. When CiCi got out of the car, he looked at the heart-shaped tag on the key, only to discover the engraving, *Love me some Amerie.* "Ah shit!" Boon exclaimed. He didn't have to explain it to CiCi, but he was feeling as though he should. He dropped the key back in the console and got out, remotely locking the car behind him. As he

83

walked up behind CiCi, he smacked her on her ass.

"Stop, fool," she said playfully, as they walked into the mall. "So this Amerie chick you talk to, how she kick it?" she asked, as they walked into Macy's.

"Nothing like you. I can't lie, CiCi, ain't none of these hoes got nothin' on Curelle." CiCi turned and Boon could sense her disbelief. "Real shit, beautiful. How you think we managed to stay so tight after all these years?" he asked.

CiCi turned down the aisle where the store stocked the Ralph Lauren collection. "Really, we been tight; 'cause you know I don't be wit' all that bullshit you be puttin' on ya skanches," she said confidently.

Boon laughed heartily, as he flashed back to when CiCi and Lil had a fight, or rather, a poor resemblance of one. CiCi had heard that Lil had been bragging about taking Boon from her and she confronted Lil, who was with a group of friends. "Aye, ho!" CiCi had yelled. Lil didn't have time to speak before CiCi was on her ass. Flurries of punches rained down on Lil's small, black face. After about three minutes of blunt force trauma to the face, CiCi was pulled off Lil. "I can have Boon if I want him, bitch. I just beat ya ass on GP because of ya mouth!" CiCi said,

as she was escorted to the principal's office.
Boon broke up with Lil two weeks later, after the
locker room incident.

CiCi and Boon spent hours in the mall, catching up on all the old times that they shared and had missed. Being with CiCi made Boon feel like a king. She hung on to his every word. She wasn't uptight with him at all, nor did she remotely give another guy any sign of interest.

"Hold up, Boon, I gotta use the ladies' room," she said, handing him two of the three shopping bags she had.

"I'ma be in the food court tryna get a couple pretzels. You want something?' Boon asked her.

"Grab me a pizza pretzel and a Coke," she said, as she walked into the restroom. Almost as soon as she entered, Boon's phone began to ring. It was Amerie calling. Boon was struck with nervousness, until he remembered that both CiCi and Amerie were only his friends. "What it is?" Boon answered the phone coolly.

"What up, baby boy? I was just checking on you to see if all was well," Amerie spoke from the other phone.

"Oh yeah, I'm good, I just thought I should grab some clothes, seeing as how I don't have any." Boon was now at the pretzel stand's counter.

"You mind grabbing a bottle of champagne or wine? I'll reimburse you when you get here."

"Champagne's on me. You already lettin' me crash in ya spot and shit," Boon replied.

"Okay; you eating with me, or don't make enough for you?" Boon thought twice about buying himself a pretzel and only motioned for the cashier to give him one pizza pretzel.

"I'm eating wit' you. I should be there shortly," Boon told her.

"No pressure. Take your time. I'm makin' smothered pork chops, yellow rice, cabbage, and cornbread. Amerie was touching a good spot in Boon. He loved soul food; especially, after Kush, and before sex.

"Okay, cool. Be there in a bit," he said and hung up the phone. He saw he had an unread text message. He checked it and saw it was from Deysha, who responded at 4:27 p.m.

Deysha: B home around 7:30. Pull up on me.

Boon looked and saw that it was presently 7:55 in the evening. He responded to the text.

Boon: I'll be there shortly.

Curelle walked up behind him, as he was ordering a second pizza pretzel for Deysha. "You 'bout ready?" she asked.

Boon handed her a pretzel and her Coke. "Yeah, I'm ready; let's go. Gotta make one stop first, if you ain't in a big hurry though." He looked at CiCi, as she shrugged her shoulders, taking a bite of her pizza pretzel as they made their way to the car.

The sun was setting on another summer night in Chicago. "CiCi," Boon began. "You believe I get jealous when I think of you and ya li'l boyfriends?"

CiCi looked at Boon, intently, and then leaned over, kissing him on his neck. "You ain't gotta be jealous, if you'd be serious, Daniel." The kiss on his neck made him stiffen, instantly, and the rest of the ride to Deysha's house was quiet, as Boon wondered if this was a better time to try CiCi for sex. The thought lingered for a few moments, and then quickly dissipated.

"I apologize if I was out of line when I gave you some of my luscious," CiCi told Boon, as he pulled into Deysha's driveway.

"You definitely got some muthafuckin' luscious, but you damn sure wasn't outta line," Boon noted. "I almost came on myself!" he exclaimed, half-jokingly.

CiCi laughed heartily, as they got out of the car. "Where we at, ol' crazy-ass boy?" CiCi paused in the driveway, as she waited for Boon, who was grabbing a Toys "R" Us bag out of the trunk.

"This is my sister's house," he answered, "and this is for my nephew." He held up the bag from the popular toy store for emphasis.

"Okay then. So that girl Deysha doing it real big now, huh?" CiCi was obviously impressed by the swanky house that his sister and her family lived in.

As Boon rang the doorbell, he responded, "This is a big-ass house, ain't it?"

Just then, the door opened. "Uncle Boon!" exclaimed Boon's nephew, Zavier. He was six years old, and always claimed that Boon was his favorite uncle; probably, because Boon always played games with him, or let him hang out with him. Unknown to Deysha, the real reason Boon let Zavier hang out with him was because he was an automatic draw for women.

"What up, 'phew? Where's Mommy?" Boon asked him.

"I'm right here. Glad you made it through, baby brother." Deysha greeted Boon with a hug. She then turned to CiCi and said, "Long time no see, girl. What the hell you and my brother doin' together?" CiCi glanced over at Boon. "Ah shit... I see. That's right, CiCi, get yo' man, girl. I don't blame you," Deysha said.

Boon handed Zavier the Toys "R" Us bag and sat on the red leather couch in the living room. CiCi sat next to him. "Sis, I can't stay long. I gotta work tomorrow. I just really missed you and intended to get around here earlier than now. But I definitely had to bring Zavier his game," Boon explained.

"That's cool; I got a surgery at eight tomorrow morning. At least you came by with yo' wife." Deysha always called Boon and CiCi husband and wife.

"Girl, yo' brother don't want no grown woman. When he leave those li'l girls alone, he knows how to find me," CiCi said.

"CiCi, I'ma take you home. Let Boon dip. We can talk about some stuff," Deysha said, making eye contact with Boon.

Boon's eyes got big, and he exclaimed, "Oh, hell naw! CiCi, let's pull. Deysha, we'll link up Friday, double-date or something." He hastily hopped up from the couch.

"Damn, bruh, I was only kidding." Deysha chuckled. "Call me so we can set up that date Friday," she said, as she walked the couple back to the door. "CiCi, get his ass, girl," she yelled, as they got back in the car.

Boon backed out of the driveway and headed back towards the interstate. "What the hell you and Deysha talking 'bout?" he asked CiCi, who was glaring out of the passenger side window, seemingly deep in thought.

"Nothing. Maybe she just knows a good fit for you when she sees one," replied CiCi, not taking her eyes off the scenery.

Boon didn't reply; he turned on Pandora Radio and, ironically, J. Holiday's "Be With Me" was playing. Boon turned up the volume and let it blast through his stereo system. He pulled up to Curelle's house and shut off the engine. "CiCi, look at me," he said. CiCi turned to Boon and they locked eyes. "You mean more to me than any of these *skanches* could ever want to mean to me. I thank you for being here for me," Boon said, solemnly.

"You better be glad I love yo' crazy-ass," CiCi said, gently, right before Boon leaned in and kissed her gently on the lips. She grabbed the back of his head, as the kiss deepened. Just when it seemed as though sparks were being set off in the car and the kiss was about to enter the next level, his phone rang. CiCi jumped back, startled a bit. She looked at the screen and saw Amerie's smiling face looking right back at her. "Ummm… catch that and call me later, Daniel," she said, blankly, as she exited the car.

"CiCi, wait," he called to no avail. CiCi kept on walking, as if she hadn't heard him calling her. He knew that she'd heard him, but he also knew that she felt some type of way about that phone call. Boon sent off a text to Amerie.

Boon: B there in 15

He sat there and watched CiCi get in the house safely before he pulled off, headed toward the liquor store. Boon purchased a bottle of Moët, hopped back in the car, and continued on to Amerie's house. He pulled up at 9:36 p.m., with a raging hard-on, courtesy of spending time with and kissing his first love.

Boon exhaled deeply, as he grabbed the shopping bags, the bottle of Moët, and the door key. He let himself in the house and noticed that there were candles lit in both the living and dining room. Amerie walked in from the kitchen with two plates, which she placed on the table. She had on a black, satin robe; and from the quick glimpse he'd gotten, she appeared to only have a bra and panties on underneath.

"Lemme take these off ya hands," she said, grabbing all the bags. He was fascinated by how smooth her skin was and she smelled like baby lotion. Boon bit his bottom lip, as he watched her walk towards her room to put away his things. He sat the champagne on the table, went into the kitchen to wash his hands, and then grabbed two champagne glasses off the rack on the counter. He sat down at the table where Amerie was already waiting.

"You gonna bless the food or should I?" Boon asked.

"I got it," she replied. They bowed their heads and she said grace.

"Damn, girl, this food is delicious. Where did you buy this?" he joked.

"Boy, bye. I cooked that on the stove by myself. I know how to cook," she scoffed.

After a few glasses of champagne, the couple was rather sauced up. They made small talk, until Amerie rose from her seat and went over to sit in Boon's lap. "Now, Mr. Boon, do you think that you can handle this?" she asked, opening her robe slightly. Boon could feel the warmth from her body on his lap, but didn't reply. He began kissing her passionately, starting with her lips, and working his way down to her cleavage. He stood up from his chair with her legs wrapped around him, and then raised her to sit on his shoulders, pinning her to the wall. He kissed her inner thighs, as she frantically worked her way out of her panties. Boon slipped his head under them and kissed her lower lips.

"Ooh!" Amerie moaned, as a shudder spiraled throughout her entire body. He stuck his tongue between her swollen lips and began using it to massage her clitoris. "Yes, baby. Right there, Boon!" Amerie ground her hips into his face, as he snaked his tongue deep into her love tunnel. He balanced her on his shoulders, using the wall for advantage, as he pulled his jogging pants down. His dick was at full attention, sensing imminent satisfaction.

"Ooh, yes, baby!" Amerie let herself go, as Boon sucked and slurped on her love box. He then eased her from his shoulders and slid her down his chest. He was about to put her down, but she slid onto the head of his dick. "Please. I want it now," she said, looking in his eyes. Boon obliged her, without breaking eye contact. She smelled her juices on his breath, as he inhaled the Moët on hers. They shared a deep, passionate kiss, as Boon worked his elongated rod into her juicy peach.

"Ah fuck!" Boon released a moan deep from within his soul.

"Oh! Oh! I knew this dick was gonna be the shit!" she exclaimed, bouncing on her way to ecstasy.

"Damn, Amerie! This pussy 'bout to make me explode!" Boon groaned, giving her hard, deep strokes.

"I want it. Don't take it out. Gimme all of it—all of it, Daddy!" Amerie bucked on his groin until she'd milked every drop Boon pumped into her. Still inside of her, Boon made his way to the couch and sat down. Amerie began kissing all over his neck and ears until he was completely aroused again. "Round two?" she asked, slowly bouncing on Boon's lap, who responded by grabbing her hips and leading the way to another orgasmic explosion.

After they were spent, they retired to a nice, steamy, hot shower together, followed by both of them falling asleep - almost instantly. The next morning, Boon got up at 7:30 sharp to get ready for work. He looked over, but Amerie was already gone. He noticed a note on her pillow that was addressed to him.

Boon, I had a wonderful time with you last night. I hope you don't think of me as a freak or think that I'm like that with every guy I meet. To be honest, I haven't been out on an actual date in four months, or had sex in six. I really like you and hope that we can pursue something a bit more serious . . . that is, of course, if you're up to it. Call me later or whatever. See, you got me thinking about that wood already, and I just got up. I'll be waiting for that call. Amerie

P.S. I made you breakfast. Hope it ain't doing too much. It's in the warmer on the stove.

Boon smiled a wide, elation-filled smile. "Shiit… you keep cookin' and fuckin' me like this, bitch gonna get a husband," he said aloud, before getting up to get ready for work. He washed up and brushed his teeth, ate, got dressed, and grabbed his phone to check the time. He saw he had an unread message from CiCi.

CiCi: Hope you didn't get 2 her 2 late. G'nite Boon.

Hangin' & Bangin'

Boon walked out the door, dressed in a Roberto Cavalli suit and Mauri gators with the eyes still in them. He was as sharp as a tack and felt like it. Getting in the car, he quickly pulled out of the driveway, and instructed his phone to call CiCi.

"What's up, Daniel?" she answered. Boon could tell she had an attitude; he'd known her way too long not to know.

"Hey, baby," he said, trying to smooth her over.

"I see you're safe. You didn't call last night; ya li'l girlfriend rushed you home, didn't she?" CiCi's voice had a sarcastic tone to it. Boon smirked to himself, as he turned onto the highway headed toward his office.

"I had to take her door key back, baby. You know you the only girl for me, CiCi," Boon lied.

"Hmmph," she scoffed. "Well, anyway, are we going to link up with Deysha this weekend, or are you leaving me and her hangin' for ya new li'l boo thang?"

"We goin', Curelle. You and Deysha need to stop plottin' on me, though. I'm in a very vulnerable state right now," he said, solemnly.

Unbeknownst to CiCi, he was actually being truthful.

"We not, Boon, but you have to be honest; we have watched you go through many trials and tribulations with these women. The hard part isn't loving you; it's having to step back and let you be a man," she said with sincerity.

"I can honestly say I understand that," he stated. "I thank y'all for loving me, and to show it, whatever you and Deysha put together, count me in." He exited the freeway and headed Downtown.

"You sure?" CiCi's voice sounded like she was up to some kind of trickery. Boon thought, for a brief minute, that perhaps he should change his mind. He realized that CiCi didn't have any malice in her heart for him, so he told her, "I'm certain." They said their goodbyes and then hung up.

Boon was feeling exceptionally well. He'd had a wonderful night with Amerie, and now, his first love seemed to want back in. As he parked his car in front of his office, his good mood was beginning to be tested. His thoughts of the two, decent women jocking for his attention was wrestling with those of the devilish trollops of his tattered past. "Damn them hoes! Fuck up a wet dream!" he muttered.

He gathered his thoughts, got out of his car, and slowly walked up towards the glass double doors. In the glass, the stenciled etching, *Watson and Holman, Attorneys at Law*, was clearly visible. Boon had opened a firm, jointly, with an old classmate, Tayshun Holman, who was from Toledo, Ohio. Tayshun and Boon shared similar physical characteristics; he was six foot tall and stocky like Boon, but he had big, dark brown eyes. He had worked with Boon at another law firm and they'd discussed going into business for themselves. They each had a stellar career and neither one of them had ever lost a case. They were criminal attorneys and were doing quite well.

Boon walked in past their receptionist's desk, where he reached behind the counter, as he always did and retrieved his messages. There were six of them, all potential clients. He glanced over them, as he strode to his office. Once he made it over to his cherry oak desk, he took off his suit coat and sat in his leather chair. He looked through the messages, again, to see what kind of charges these potential clients were facing.

The very first card he came across immediately caught his attention. Taibachi Stover's charges made Boon's eyes bulge. His charges were possession of a firearm by a convicted felon, trafficking and aggravated assault on a police officer. "Damn! Whoever this mu'fucka is, he wasn't playin'," Boon murmured. He put an asterisk on the card and perused the other five. After reading all six cards, Boon put them in order from the higher profiled to the least profiled. Before he had a chance to pick up the phone to return any phone calls, the buzzer on the intercom sounded, letting him know that Kayla was calling.

"Kayla, what's going on?" Boon asked.

"Good morning, boss man," Kayla greeted him. "You have an unscheduled consultation request. Are you available, or should I set them an appointment?" Makayla Gordon had come highly referenced when she applied for the job at Boon's law firm. Her credentials were impeccable and she had a great attitude. She was short, heavy-set, and had a cocoa brown complexion. What she lacked in height, she more than made up in confidence. Her beauty and intelligence afforded her more than her share of gentlemen callers.

Boon frowned at the phone. *Kayla knows that I don't accept walk-ins.* "Make an appointment. No, wait; take a message and I'll call them in a couple minutes." He sat up and prepared to hang up when he heard Kayla speak again.

"Actually, Mr. Watson, she's here in the office already."

What the hell? Kayla knows that I don't take walk-ins, he thought, again. *Especially, females.*

"Uh, I guess you can send her in, Kayla." Boon was looking down at his message cards, when his door opened. "Have a seat. I'll be with you in just a second," he said, without lifting his head. The woman sat across from him in one of the two leather chairs in front of his desk. He sniffed the air and realized he recognized the fragrance. "Flowerbomb. It's a rather intoxicating fragrance," he said.

"You should know, you bought it for me," the familiar voice said from across the desk. Boon looked up and saw a face he hoped that he would never see again. Like it or not, he was now face-to-face with Taz.

"What the fuck are you doing here?" he hissed, looking at her with hatred in his eyes. The gash on the side of his head began to throb, as a reminder of the attack he'd suffered because of this treacherous woman.

"Lemme at least tell you what happened before you assume anything, Daniel," Taz said, not caring about Boon's apparent displeasure.

"You got some muthafuckin' nerve, waltzing your triflin'-ass in here. Gimme one good reason not to break your neck myself." Boon stood up and walked towards Taz; she stood up as well, and pulled a .22 out of her purse. Boon halted in his tracks when he saw the revolver in her hand. "Oh, so you finna shoot me now?"

Taz raised her eyebrow. "Pearl is strictly for protection. Now, sit down, Boon. We have somethin' to talk about," Taz answered, as she motioned with the gun for him to have a seat. She sat down as well, adjusting her jade-colored dress that stopped just above her knees, with a split up the side that showed off her plentiful thighs. Boon reluctantly took his seat, feeling like a sucker now, because not only did she get the drop on him, he was actually getting aroused looking at her.

"You a dirty bitch, Taz. Fuckin' dirty!" he sternly whispered.

"I woulda loved to hear that when you was all up in me, but now it just makes you look like a pussy." Taz sat the gun in her lap, evidently, more comfortable now that Boon was seated. She fumbled around in a Michael Kors handbag that matched the color of her dress and pulled out a picture. "First of all, Boon, I didn't have you set up to be robbed, shot, attacked, or none of that shit," she commented.

Boon sat back in his chair and clasped his hands together on his desk. "I find that extremely hard to believe, Tatiyana," he said, as calmly as possible.

"Nigga, I loved your stupid-ass. Why the fuck would I do some dumbass shit like that?" she retorted, just as calm.

Boon twisted his lips, as if she really knew the answer already, but he answered anyway. "Because your loyalty lies wherever the money is and that's the worst kind of person to me."

Taz dropped her head. "Boon, I know I'm not the woman of most men's dreams. Yes, I look good, but my mom had it rough with broke-ass men and I didn't want any parts of that. Look, you were my first love; it was immature of me to leave you for money. It definitely wasn't for the little dick nigga who had it." Taz looked up at Boon. "I pay for that every day now. I wanted to be yours forever, have you some little Boons and grow old with you." They both let a small smile creep across their faces, at the mention of children.

"So, how we go from fuckin' each other's brains out, to me getting this?" he asked, pointing to his stitches.

"There's a nigga named Anterious. Everybody calls him Swank. I used to date his brother, Angelo. Angelo got 25 years for trafficking, armed robbery and involuntary manslaughter." Taz sat the picture she was holding on the desk. "This is a dude named Tavius that I was cheating on Angelo with. He was also an undercover police officer that used me to help get Angelo put away. Swank told me I had to help him get a lawyer to file his brother's appeal, one way or another." Taz took a deep breath, while Boon sat back, waiting on the punchline.

"Our night together was real, Boon. I had been with Angelo's sister the night before. Swank showed up and asked me for money on his brother's lawyer. I had already mustered up $5500, and I wasn't trying to let this bastard scare me into giving him shit else. Long story short, he must have followed me out to your place— "

Boon interrupted her. "How the hell did my door get unlocked though? I never leave my door unlocked, Tatiyana," Boon objected. Taz sat there in silence, as if she hadn't thought her lie all the way through. "You come into my establishment, after you got me attacked and robbed, trying to lie, as if you gave a fuck about

103

me breathin'? That shit was all your fault! You're worse than scum. I wouldn't piss on you if you were on fire, Taz!" Boon's voice was full of venom. "Fuck you, your community pussy, and that li'l punk-ass peashooter in your lap, bitch! Now, see ya way up outta my shit!" Boon stood and faced the window.

"Daniel, I'm lost. I don't know what to do," Taz's voice was shaky. "Why the hell can't I get a good man? Why is it that men only want to fuck me or get their dicks sucked?"

Boon continued to look out the window and stated, "Those are your only valuable assets and that's sad. Now, get the fuck away from me, before I have your scandalous-ass arrested." He waved his hand in a dismissive manner to emphasize his point.

Taz stared at his back, hopelessly, for a few moments before collecting herself and walking to the door. She paused, as she grabbed the knob; and without turning around, she said, "It wasn't gonna get no better than me. All your women fuck you over, ol' lame-ass nigga."

Boon chuckled. "And niggas only fuck you. I got a check—long money. Fuck you think got me in yo' mouth again? Don't let the Esquire title fool you, Taz. I'm still a street nigga. Take care of that pussy though; it's the only thing that's gon' get yo' gold-diggin'-ass paid." Taz walked out and slammed the door behind her. Boon lit a Cuban cigar and sat back in his desk chair to calm his nerves, before making his business calls.

By 4:30 p.m., Boon had decided to take on all six of the cases. He ran them by Tayshun, who agreed. Earlier in the day, he'd spoken to Amerie and they agreed to meet up at Burger King for a light dinner, before going to bowl a few frames. He hopped in his car, listening to a hot, new artist, A.I. Da CroweMan's mixtape. His groove was suddenly interrupted by an incoming call from an unknown number. Boon started not to answer, but since it may have been business, he did.

"Hello. This is Daniel Watson," he said, with his professional swagger on.

"Can I at least take you to dinner before I go back home? Everything is on me," the voice on the other end offered.

Boon looked at the number on the screen again. "Who is this?" he asked.

"This is Zo, Boon. I know I ain't on ya VIP list of people you want to talk to right now, but I come in peace," she said.

He contemplated the offer for a moment. "What you got in mind, Ms. Tucker?"

"How 'bout we step away from the uppity and grab some Mexican, a drink or two, then hit a comedy club? I hear DeRay Davis is in town," she suggested.

"You know what? You got yourself a date, Zo." Boon surprised himself with his answer. Zo was on that list of people he wouldn't miss if he never saw them again. "So, where do I need to be and what time?" he asked.

"If you don't mind ridin' in my Camry, I'll just come get you around 8," she gushed.

Boon knew it wouldn't be good looks to have another woman meet him at Amerie's house. "I'll just meet you where you want me to, Zo. I got a couple errands to run."

"That's fine. Meet me at our old hangout Downtown at 8. I'll be waiting." Boon agreed and ended the call.

When Boon arrived at the house, he told Amerie that they had to reschedule their date. She tried to hide the fact that she was in her feelings about him cancelling on her to go out with some friends, but Boon saw it. He showered, dressed and told himself, *it's all good; we're just friends, right?* Deep down inside, though, he knew he was wrong as hell.

He strolled through the house and was at the door when he turned to tell Amerie he'd see her later on. He walked back towards her and hugged her. She gave him a deep squeeze as well, murmuring, "Umm… you smell so good." Amerie rolled her hips against him, as she held on tightly.

"Alright now!" Boon said, watching her lick her lips provocatively. He exhaled sharply to clear the sexy thoughts running through his mind.

"I may be up when you get back. If not, you can wake me up, if you wanna." She winked, as she walked away seductively.

The ride to Fiesta Mexicana was a short one. Boon pulled up in the parking lot, and the memories came flooding back from when he and Zo were college students at DePaul. He walked in and, instantly, felt more relaxed in the familiar surroundings.

"Sir," a young, Hispanic waitress called for his attention. "There's a young lady waving for you to come over." The waitress pointed to a table not far from the bar. Zo was wearing her hair down, dyed honey blonde, with sandy streaks. The color complemented her creamy white complexion perfectly.

"Hello, beautiful," Boon greeted her when he reached the table. He leaned in and kissed her on the cheek, before sliding into the seat across the table from her.

"Hello, handsome. Well, don't you look rather . . . Boon-ish." She referred to the nice threads that he'd earned a reputation for wearing.

After eating, a few drinks, and reminiscing about the good, old days, Zo suggested that he follow her to park her car at her hotel. "It doesn't make sense for us to drive two cars. I can park mine, and we can ride in yours."

Boon was agreeable to her plan; especially, since she had been gracious enough to pay for everything and was on her best behavior. They got into their respective cars, dropped her car off, and she settled into Boon's plush, leather, passenger seat. As soon as she clicked her seatbelt, Boon pulled off, headed for the Laugh Factory.

They entered the comedy club, paid their entrance fee, and were escorted to their seats, which were close enough to the stage to hear, but not close enough for the comedians to poke fun at them. DeRay Davis didn't disappoint them, and they laughed their asses off, sharing a few drinks there as well. Boon was enjoying himself more than he thought he would. Not to mention, Zo hadn't brought up her son at all during their date.

Walking back to his car, Boon realized they were holding hands. He felt it would be more awkward to let go now, so he continued to hold hers. He made sure that she was in the car safely, and then he entered his car for the ride back to her room.

Both Boon and Zo were silent on the way back. It slowly began to rain. The drops pitter-pattered along the windshield until they turned into a full-fledged deluge. Boon clicked on his wipers and adjusted his speed accordingly.

"How's work been, Boon? I never got the chance to ask." Zo broke the silence.

Boon automatically thought back to the encounter he had with Taz earlier in the day. He smirked, as he started speaking. "It's been eventful, to say the least." He glanced briefly at Zo. Her tanned skin was flawless and she had on a minimal amount of makeup. She allowed her natural beauty to shine through. She made eye contact with him, and when he turned his head, her eyes took in his immaculately-lined goatee. She decided to go in for the kill.

"Boon, I'm leaving this weekend and I have a lot of people to catch up with. Would it be asking too much of you to spend the rest of the night with me?"

The light just ahead of them turned red, and Boon rolled to a stop, two blocks away from the hotel. He had a serious buzz going, and Zo's hypnotic fragrance and enthralling beauty held him captive. "I'm glad you offered. I don't wanna be driving drunk in this rain all fuckin' night," he said, as soon as the light turned green.

Zo smiled, softly, elated that she would have a chance at convincing Boon to give *them* another go. Boon parked his car right beside hers in the Hilton Chicago's lot. Zo used her keycard to let them into her Lakeview Suite and the aroma of fresh, linen-scented potpourri filled their nostrils. "That's my shit right there though!" she exclaimed, doing a little two-step into the room. Meek Mill's "I'ma Boss" video was playing on BET. She'd left the widescreen TV on when she'd left to go meet Boon at the restaurant.

After closing the door behind him, Boon's eyes scanned the room. The incident with Taz, at his house, had made him much more aware of his surroundings.

"Honey, you good in here; I promise." Zo kicked off her Chanel sandals and headed into the bathroom.

Boon snatched up the remote and turned on a movie. He removed his chocolate Timbs and sat all the way back on the bed. He could hear the shower and a small radio playing. *Ain't smoked no bud in a few weeks; wonder if I still got some in my stash?* "Aye, Zo, I'm 'bout to run to the car right quick," Boon yelled through the bathroom door. He grabbed the keycard off the nightstand, shoved his feet back into his boots, and headed towards the door.

"You gonna come back up though, right?" Zo hollered back.

Boon laughed. "Yeah, girl. Right back." He went to the car and got his stash, but then he realized that his blunts were stale, so he dashed to the convenience store and purchased a few. Twenty minutes later, he returned with some fresh Dutches and about four grams of Kush. He opened the door to a red glow illuminating throughout the room. Zo was sitting naked on the bed, the pungent smell of her Victoria's Secret lotion permeating the air. He sat on the bed in front of her and began to break down the Dutch.

Zo sat up on her knees behind him and began massaging his shoulders. "Hold up, before you do that. Put a wet towel under the door. You know these people trip off the weed smoke," Boon said.

She slid off the bed to grab the towel out of the restroom, and as she walked by, Boon leaned over and softly bit her on her ass cheek.

"Ohh," she hissed, startled from the bite. "All right, boy," she warned, as she strolled into the bathroom.

Boon lay back on the bed and lit the spliff. He took a deep, strong pull and held the smoke in his lungs. Zo returned to the bed and positioned herself so her breasts were pressed against Boon's arms. Her nipples began to harden, just from his masculinity alone.

"Damn, that shit stank so good!" she exclaimed, when Boon exhaled.

"True dat," he replied, passing her the blunt. She grabbed the blunt and straddled Boon's stomach. Her vagina was throbbing and he could feel its wetness. His penis became harder than Chinese arithmetic. "Damn! I do miss givin' yo' sexy-ass the business."

Boon ran his hands lightly up her stomach and gracefully across her breasts. Her juices began to flow, profusely, and she tried to pass him the blunt. He pointed to the ashtray above his head, and as she leaned forward, her abdomen was touching his nose. He began planting sensual kisses on her torso, while he worked his way out of his jeans.

Zo reached back and grabbed his erect wood; he was more than ready. She climbed off the bed and pulled her hair into a ponytail, right before she went to work on the stiff rod waving from his midsection.

Hot damn, she could suck a watermelon through a water hose, he thought.

Boon wrapped his hand in her ponytail, and began using her head as a plunger. She was loving every minute of him enjoying her. She knew it was just a matter of seconds before he'd blast off. Zo snatched a condom out her nightstand drawer and put it on Boon's pole.

Position after position, they energetically sexed each other until they both tapped out, sweaty beyond belief. Boon couldn't remember her ever being this juiced up for him. He hadn't even realized until they were sexing doggy style that she had BOON tatted across her ass cheeks. She was everything Boon needed; or she *was* at least, until she sat up and said, "Boon, please let me have you."

Although they were in the dark and could barely see each other, he looked at Zo as though she knew better. He remained silent as she continued. "I mean, it ain't like we ain't got

113

chemistry, Boon. And you still fuck me like you miss me." She got closer to him and kissed his ear. "Don't you want me too, baby?" she asked.

The *baby* part sent Boon in the wrong direction, and he broke his silence. "Not like you want me to want you."

Zo sat up, immediately, with an attitude. "What the fuck does that mean? So, I'm good enough to fuck and suck you, but ain't no room for me to belong to you?" she asked. "I swear men ain't shit! You dirty, for real!"

"Me? Dirty?" Boon sat up also. "You gotta be out yo' rabbit-ass mind! Y'all hoes ain't shit; at least you hoes I stick my dick in. I swear, y'all think this shit somethin' to play wit'!" He shouted.

"Fuck you, Boon. You selfish son of a bitch!" Zo got up off the bed and threw his clothes in his face. "Get the fuck out! I'm glad my son ain't come from you. At least he won't be a womanizing, arrogant fuck, like the man who shoulda been his father."

She had struck a nerve, making Boon jump up naked to confront her. "Bitch, I should shoot you in yo' muthafuckin' face. You know good and damn well I wanted that to be my boy!" he screamed in her face.

"So, you saying we can fuck and make babies, but not have a relationship?" she yelled back.

"That's exactly what the fuck I'm saying!"

"You ain't shit, Boon!"

"Ol' dizzy-ass woman! Ain't no relationship because yo' whorish-ass went dick-hoppin' and made a baby on me with God knows who." Boon slid into his pants and boots, putting on his shirt and grabbing his keys. He yelled, "Zora Tucker, fuck you, yo' son, and yo' life! Don't hit my line ever again! I'm out this muthafucka!"

Zo began to cry angry tears and ran through the room. She jumped on Boon's back, punching him in the back of his head. She was cursing and screaming so hard, the only thing he could make out was, "Don't you dare walk out that door," as the blows continued to rain on his skull.

"Ho, get yo' stupid-ass off me!" Boon yelled, effortlessly tossing her to the bed. She broke down weeping, but Boon didn't give a fuck. "Good fuckin' riddance," he shouted, leaving the room and slamming the door behind him.

"Choosy Lover"

Several months passed by and Boon was in full stride. He had won four of the six cases that he had taken to trial, and was currently working on the last two. In the last two months, he had finally moved into a three-bedroom house in Joliet, Illinois, just south of Chicago. When asked about the choice in house size, he'd just shrug and say, "You never know." He and Amerie were still on good terms and were constantly going out on dates to several different places. She was growing on him and he could feel himself wanting something bigger with her, but one big thing was holding him back—CiCi.

CiCi had also re-emerged as a force to be reckoned with in Boon's life. When he wasn't working, his time was split, evenly, between her and Amerie. He seemed to have more fun with CiCi, because she already knew him, so they were connected on every level. Well, almost every level. CiCi was no longer a virgin, but was still hesitant to let Boon conquer her pussy. She knew he was very well endowed and that he did love her, but she loved him deeper. CiCi wasn't sure Boon was ready to fully commit to any one woman, and that made her apprehensive.

Boon was at his desk in his former den, now turned office, going over some notes for his current client's case when his phone rang. It was Deysha.

"What up, sister?" Boon asked, as he placed the call on speaker.

"Baby brother, you at home?" she asked.

"Yeah. Just now going over this Montford case. What's the deal?" Boon quizzed.

"Shit; I'm taking a couple weeks off. Wanna smoke for old time's sake?" Deysha chuckled a little. She felt like she was still in high school, hiding the fact that she smoked marijuana from their parents.

"Come through. I need a break anyway," Boon said.

"Okay. I got CiCi wit' me, if you don't mind?" Deysha asked.

Of course, Boon didn't ever mind CiCi coming. *Her and Deysha had been spending a lot of time together lately.*

"You know she good, sis. That's my nigga," Boon stated.

"Didn't know if you had company or not, bruh, but we on the way."

Boon was confused by that statement, but let it go. He ended the call and went to straighten up the house a bit. It wasn't dirty, but he'd just done his laundry and his clothes were in the living room, where he had been watching the Bears beating the brakes off the Vikings.

An hour and a half later, Boon's doorbell rang, while he was deep-frying some whiting fillets and some homemade hush puppies. He looked out the peephole and saw Deysha's smiling face. He wiped his hands on a towel he'd draped over his shoulder and opened the door.

"Hey, baby brother!" Deysha yelled, as if it had been ages since they'd last seen each other. She was dressed in a Marc Jacobs, denim jeans and jacket combo with a grey turtleneck on under it. When she hugged Boon, he could tell it was cold outside from the coolness of her cheeks. CiCi was behind her with a white, Donna Karan sweater on top of a red, form-fitting, Donna Karan pencil skirt. She had on four-inch, red, Donna Karan heels to match. What really took Boon's breath, was how her hips looked in the skirt. CiCi stepped up to hug him and got lost in the moment. Boon kissed her on her lips gently. After stepping back, their eyes were fixed on each other. CiCi was taken off guard by the welcomed display of affection, but it warmed her like a shot of tequila.

"Ahem," Deysha cleared her throat. "Can we get this party started, you two?" she asked.

Boon turned and walked in the kitchen to check on his fish and hush puppies.

"Make yourselves at home. Well, y'all know that already," he said, on his way back to the kitchen.

"Boy, it smells good as a mu'fucka in there." CiCi said, dropping her jacket on the couch and making her way to the kitchen. "I could get used to this," she said, seeing Boon on his chef shit at the stove.

"I hope to see it become so, one day," Boon said, as he watched her walk towards him.

"Boon, stop playing with me, boy. Besides, yo' li'l skanchy ain't gon' let you leave her alone," CiCi said and walked towards the fridge.

"Whatever," Boon said seriously. "Can you watch the food for me? I gotta use the bathroom and grab the weed." He didn't wait for an answer.

Boon relieved himself and went to his room to grab the Kush. He brought out a cutie, seven grams, and his favorite Dutch Masters. CiCi had taken the food from the deep fryer and was letting the paper towels soak up the grease.

"Deysha, roll 'em fat too. Yo' ass be rollin' them sewing needles and shit," Boon poked fun.

"You know I don't get to party like you," Deysha said, defensively.

"Boon, yo' phone ringing over here." CiCi pointed at his phone, sliding across the table. It was on vibrate from earlier when he had the radio extremely loud. "Ah shit! It's yo' wife," CiCi said, half-jokingly.

"I'll call her later." Boon continued to breakdown some weed.

"Man, answer the phone, Boon. We just fuckin' wit' you," CiCi said.

Deysha got up and grabbed the ringing phone off the table.

"Hello?" she answered.

Amerie had only ever heard Boon answer his cell, so she was caught off guard.

"Um… is...uh... Boon...I mean, Daniel available?" she stammered.

Deysha fought back her laugh.

"Yes he is; but first, when do I get to meet you?" Deysha asked.

She was now running around the table, trying to avoid Boon, who was chasing her for the phone.

"May I ask who I'm speaking with?" Amerie quizzed.

After realizing he would not be able to catch her, Boon went to finish rolling the blunts.

"Damn, you got to try to hide us from the broad too, Daniel?" CiCi said, once Boon sat down. Deysha was still talking to Amerie. Boon ignored CiCi's comment and continued rolling up. "I guess I'm out of place asking 'bout ya li'l friend." CiCi got up and went towards the back of the house.

Boon looked towards his sister in disbelief.

"What the hell you mean, 'we'll see you in a few then'?" Boon asked with attitude.

"We wanna meet this chick you spending all ya time wit'," Deysha said, walking to the couch where Boon was seated. "It ain't like you and CiCi in a relationship. Yo' punk-ass is scared of a real woman."

Deysha wanted Boon and CiCi together. For the second time, Boon looked incredulously at his sister.

"I don't know what the hell y'all got goin' on, but y'all ain't finna play volleyball wit' my dick though!" Boon felt some type of way about Deysha trying to direct his love life.

"I could care less about the li'l skanch. I love my potna and wanna meet who got him all wrapped up when I don't hear from him," CiCi said, as she emerged from the hallway.

It was CiCi that now got a disbelieving stare from Boon.

"Man, me and you are always together. Do you tell Deysha that?" Boon was feeling annoyed and double-teamed. Deysha and CiCi were about to reply simultaneously, but Boon cut them off. "Wait," he said, raising his hand. "I don't owe either one of y'all any type of explanation about a muthafuckin' thang Daniel does! So, if we gon' chill, smoke and talk shit, that is what the fuck needs to happen. Otherwise, both of y'all can get the hell out. No offense," he said. Both Deysha and CiCi remained silent, as he lit the L. "Good," Boon said, as he took a deep toke of the strong marijuana, before sitting back on the couch.

Thirty minutes into the smoke session, Boon's phone rang. Deysha and CiCi both looked at him, but stayed still.

"Oh, don't act like y'all can't answer my shit now," Boon said to them both.

Deysha was the one to grab the phone. "Hello?" she said, without checking the caller ID.

"I'm in your driveway. Is it okay to come in?" Amerie sounded uncertain.

"Yeah. The door already unlocked," Deysha said, with very little enthusiasm.

He and his sister was eating, while CiCi was rolling another blunt. The motion sensor chimed to let them know that someone was coming in. Amerie stepped through and closed the door behind her. She was dressed in Burberry denim jeans, Burberry skippers, and a Burberry coat. Beneath the skullcap she was wearing, her glistening hair was hanging down.

"Hello, everyone," she greeted, as she began to take her coat off.

Deysha and CiCi got up to introduce themselves. Deysha was stunned by Amerie's beauty and felt that the picture in her brother's phone did Amerie's up close and personal features no justice.

"Amerie, what's good? I'm Deysha," she extended her hand.

"Okay. Nice to finally meet Daniel's favorite sibling," Amerie said solemnly. Deysha blushed, although she already knew she was Boon's favorite. CiCi stepped up to introduce herself, but before she could, Amerie said, "CiCi. Nice to make your acquaintance. I've heard so much about you."

CiCi was caught off guard by this. "Oh, my. Nice to meet you as well, Amerie. Can't really say that I've heard much about you," CiCi lied.

Boon looked at CiCi, wondering what the hell she was up to. It was like water on leather the way Amerie let the comment roll off her. She felt as though CiCi liked Boon as more than a friend, but wasn't about to stand down from her conquest—Boon as her husband.

Surprisingly, the situation had been a decent one. No trouble was brewing. Deysha wasn't instigating any gratuitous quarrels between Amerie and CiCi. Amerie was cool and very talkative with CiCi and Deysha. CiCi hadn't been smarting Amerie as Boon had been expecting her to. The quartet was having fun and Boon's anxiety about the evening quickly dissipated.

"Anybody want a daiquiri?" Deysha asked. She got a simultaneous chorus of yes's from the entire room. "Boon, you got what we need?" she asked her brother, as she went to the kitchen.

"Yep. Liquor under the bar, as well as Mike's. Blender next to microwave and plenty ice; you know where." Boon told her. "Aye, y'all wanna play spades?" Boon asked the ladies.

Amerie was rolling a blunt. Surprisingly, to everyone, including Boon, she knew how to roll up.

"Who on teams?" Deysha asked.

Boon, still avoiding any type of situation that may occur, said, "Sis, me and you gon' be on teams."

Amerie didn't mind playing on CiCi's team, but it seemed like CiCi was shocked at the fact that Boon didn't want to be on her team. Nevertheless, she rolled with the punches.

The game was tied and Amerie wanted to win this one badly. Deysha and Boon had already beaten them twice.

"So, Amerie, what you do for a living?" Deysha asked, before taking a swig of her second strawnana daiquiri. Boon was smoking a blunt, as CiCi dealt the cards.

"I'm a lawyer," she answered, after taking a swallow of her second fuzzy navel daiquiri.

Deysha had whipped up four kinds, because she didn't know who would want what. There was fuzzy navel, strawnana, which was a strawberry and banana mixture, piña colada, and apple mimosa. Boon was halfway through his third and he'd had all the flavors, except the piña colada.

"Oh, so you and my brother got that in common." Deysha commented.

"CiCi, what do you do?"

CiCi was done dealing and reaching for the blunt from Boon, when Amerie asked the question.

"I'm a guidance counselor at an elementary school," CiCi replied.

"Oh," Amerie said, plainly, with a look on her face that said, *that's it?* Amerie went a step further. "Where did you and Boon meet?" Amerie asked and Deysha choked on her drink.

Boon was about to interject, but CiCi was already standing up.

"Bitch, that ain't nunna yo' business," she spat.

Amerie, still seated, was unfazed by the comment. "Well, damn. You mad or nah? I just asked a simple fuckin' question," Amerie said, just before taking a sip of her drink.

"Mad? Nah, I ain't mad. I just don't like nosy bitches asking questions about *my* fuckin' business!" CiCi was getting pissed with every exchanged comment.

"Yo' business? From what I hear, yo' business ain't got shit to do with Boon, so I don't see why knowing where y'all met was a problem. I mean, it ain't like y'all fucked, or are fucking," Amerie said.

Boon jumped up in time to catch CiCi before she could get to the other side of the table. Amerie still didn't budge.

"Man, what the fuck y'all got goin' on? We was just chillin' and y'all startin' to act like teenagers and shit," Boon scolded.

CiCi looked at him incredulously.

"Boon, fuck you and yo' Barbie doll. Fuck you mean, 'what we got goin' on'? You should be asking ya li'l fuck toy over there." CiCi felt tears of anger welling up in her eyes.

"I'll proudly be his fuck toy, you uptight, pompous, save-the-worst-for-last-pussy-havin'-ass bitch. Maybe you shoulda given our boy some of that pussy, wit' yo' thick for nothin' ass!" Amerie had spunk. In a way, it was turning Boon on. Deysha was shocked and speechless. Boon had relaxed his grip on CiCi, not thinking she would continue to try to get at Amerie. CiCi stiff pushed Boon so hard, he flipped over his chair. She hopped over the fallen Boon as Amerie jumped from her seat. From her BCBG clutch, Amerie brandished her .38. CiCi stopped in her tracks, when she saw the pistol. "I'ma peaceful bitch, CiCi, but make no mistakes about it, I'm from AG. I came to have fun, but I see you can't play nice," Amerie said, with the gun pointed at CiCi.

"Amerie, what the fuck, ma?" Boon hollered, getting up off the floor.

Deysha was still quiet and seemingly glued to her seat. CiCi didn't want to find out how gangsta Amerie was, at least not while she was holding the gun. She stood still, hoping she wouldn't shoot. Amerie stepped backwards, still pointing the gun at CiCi. She grabbed her coat and skully, and then continued to walk backwards towards the front door.

"Boon, she fine as hell, but she ain't me, baby. This pussy only wants you; so, when you ready, call me. I'll be waiting. CiCi, sorry we couldn't end this night as friends. Deysha, thanks for the invite and for being neutral." Amerie said, walking out the door and closing it behind her. CiCi exhaled a long breath she seemed to have been holding since Amerie pulled the gun.

"Bruh, that ho wild. She always got that banger on her?" Deysha broke the silence.

Before Boon could respond, CiCi turned and smacked fire from his ass.

"How dare you talk about us to this new bitch, Daniel; is that what you do, huh?"

Boon shook away some of the stars he saw before saying, "CiCi, I told her who you were, and she just asked if we had ever slept together. I gave her an honest answer." Boon's face felt like he was lying on burning coal.

"If I see the bitch again, I'm killing her," CiCi said. Boon was livid. Not only did he not have an idea how things got out of hand, he'd also gotten the shit slapped out of him behind it. "If you gon' fuck wit' her, don't call me no mo'

128

either; especially, since she down to fuck and I want you to be a man first," CiCi screamed.

"How the hell you gon' sit here and gimme an ultimatum? I don't owe you shit, Curelle. Fuck you talkin' 'bout!" Boon lost it. "Fuck all y'all! Deysha, take her home. Now!" Boon walked off.

CiCi was now weeping, as she stepped to the kitchen for a couple of paper towels to dry her face.

"Boon, don't do me like that!" CiCi sobbed. "I only wanted us to be. Instead of trying, you always got some new bitch you got to tell me about!" CiCi sobbed.

Deysha was following Boon towards his bedroom.

"Boon, will you— " Boon slammed his door in her face.

"Deysha, take CiCi home. I'ma fuck wit' y'all some other time." Boon spat from behind the closed bedroom door.

Deysha understood her brother's frustration, so she left him alone. She walked back to the kitchen to check on CiCi.

"Before you say anything, Deysha, I'm okay. I just wanna leave." CiCi walked out of the kitchen and grabbed her coat.

Deysha didn't push for any more answers.

CiCi was quiet the entire ride back to the city. All she could think of was high school and not giving in to Boon's hormones. She wished she had given him what she knew they both wanted. Boon was stubborn as a mule, and this was the only time she'd ever hit him. CiCi questioned whether slapping him was warranted.

"Deysha," she said, with her voice cracking. "Was I wrong? I mean, for anything I did tonight? And don't sugarcoat nothin'."

Deysha sighed. "Over time, hell no. Tonight though, I think you overreacted slightly," she replied.

CiCi's eyes were red and glossy from crying. She pulled out her phone and sent Boon a text message.

CiCi: **I'm sorry, Daniel. Guess the best woman won.**

When she sent the text, she asked Deysha, "What do you think is gonna happen now?"

Deysha shook her head. "When Boon last did what he just did, no one in the family heard from him until almost eight months later. I usually can get him to talk to me, but he has his ways." Deysha glanced at CiCi, briefly. "Honestly, you may have run him straight to her. We shall soon find out though."

CiCi listened, as she looked out the passenger window at the scenery. She wished she could relive the moments that led up to the altercation. She loved Boon more than she cared to tell anyone. Her eyes began to tear up at the thought of losing him. Deysha rubbed CiCi's thigh in an attempt to console her. As CiCi wiped the tears from her face, her phone vibrated. It was an incoming text from Boon.

Boon: U know I want u and u want me. Stop acting tough and come back. ALONE.

CiCi smiled on the inside, as Deysha noticed a mood change in CiCi's face.

"What is it?" Deysha wondered, aloud.

After she texted Boon that she'd be back to his house by 10:00 p.m. sharp, she said to Deysha, "I got a date tonight." Deysha couldn't fathom with who it could've been, but she was happy CiCi wasn't crying anymore. "Let's stop by Victoria's Secret before you take me to my house," CiCi said with a smile.

"Ah, shit! Girl, who finna get lucky and hit that phat ass tonight?" Deysha inquired.

CiCi smiled harder, more devilishly this time. "I'ma tell you; I just can't until it's done. Bitch, my pussy is throbbin' just thinkin' about it," she said.

Deysha drove on without a clue.

Payback

It was very busy in the Downtown Chicago shopping district. Some people were doing some last minute Valentine's shopping, while others just walked through the stores and boutiques, window-shopping and killing time. Deysha was a big spender; especially, when it came to name brands; but today, she was focused more on CiCi's sudden emotional change. She didn't have any compunctions about it, but she did find it rather strange how quickly CiCi went from a sobbing mess, to smiling and store hopping for lingerie.

"So you really not finna tell me who you 'bout to smash, huh?" she asked CiCi, when they walked into Victoria's Secret.

CiCi smiled provocatively at Deysha and batted her eyelashes. "FYI, I just wanna keep this one to myself for now. Let me relish in the moment, girl," CiCi said.

"Whatever, trick," Deysha replied.

CiCi looked at Deysha, wondering if she meant any offense.

"Deysha, why you actin' like that?" CiCi asked her.

Deysha was looking at a lavender bra and panty set she thought her husband might like to see her in. "Honestly, you and Boon kill me. He wants you, but he's scared you not gonna be wild enough. You want him, but you scared to show him he ain't gonna want another bitch," Deysha said, throwing the undies in her hand basket. "Then tonight, I watched you slap the dog shit outta my brother - any other bitch I'd have killed. You hit him because you was scared to let him top that off," Deysha said, meaning every word.

"Damn! Excuse me for wanting to be a lady and not somebody's deep freezer," CiCi said, with a little attitude in her tone.

Deysha looked her way and stopped. "Fuck you mean, 'deep freezer'?" she asked.

"You know, the pussy that niggas be usin' just to stick they meat in," CiCi replied, with a straight face.

Both women burst out laughing, causing all the store's patrons to turn their way.

After realizing that more than half of the customers in the store were gawking at them, Deysha said, "Half the bitches who shop here are somebody's deep freezer."

The pair shared another brief chuckle and continued to shop.

CiCi and Deysha finally finished shopping, after an hour and a half in the many stores they visited. CiCi had bought some red stilettos to go with the red boy shorts and bra set with black hearts all over them. She also bought a black and red Mardi Gras mask to go with it. Deysha convinced her that it would be spicy. By now, it was 8:45 and CiCi was pressed for time.

"Girl, drop me off so I can get my night poppin'," she told Deysha.

Deysha was ready to go as well.

"I wish Boon was the lucky guy tonight. You might just tighten his ass up with this one," Deysha said, backing her Maserati out of the parking space.

"Yeah, well, maybe one day he'll realize I'm supposed to be his," CiCi said, trying to throw Deysha off.

It gave her even more of an erotic feeling, just keeping it a secret from Deysha. It felt almost as if she was about to do something she wasn't supposed to do.

"I hear you. Don't hurt nobody," Deysha said, jokingly.

CiCi only smiled.

It took only 20 minutes for Deysha to get CiCi to her house, as traffic was almost a non-factor. During the entire ride, Deysha was displaying her caginess in hopes of getting CiCi to spill the beans, but to no avail. CiCi was not budging.

"Call me tomorrow, heifer, and let me know how tonight plays out for you and this lucky mu'fucka," Deysha said, as CiCi got out of the coupe in her driveway.

"I might," CiCi said, ending their day of fun and revelry.

Deysha watched CiCi make it safely into the house, before pulling off.

CiCi hadn't made it in the house good before she had gotten a text from Boon.

Boon: **Bring a box of Dutches ...if you still comin' thru.**

Of course she was still coming. She texted back to let Boon know just that. CiCi brushed her teeth and hair, but opted to shower at Boon's house when she got there. She did not want to keep him waiting. He had already waited for more than 10 years.

"Okay, CiCi. You can handle this. You've been in love with this man since you were 14." She gave herself a pep talk in the bathroom mirror. CiCi knew she wouldn't be back home tonight, so she packed an overnight bag as well. She checked her home phone's answering machine, just as she was about to walk out of her bedroom. There was only one message, and had she known whom it was from prior to listening, she would have erased it without a second thought.

"Aye, sexy," the message began. "....this is Rollo. I know you miss a nigga. Let me have you tonight, so we can watch the sunrise together."

Rollo was CiCi's first and she thought he was the one; especially, since Boon was whore-hopping around that time. Rollo met his demise in CiCi's heart when she found out that he had fucked two of her co-workers when she was working at the airport. She had given him her number two weeks ago after running into him at Walmart.

"Negro, puh-lease!" she spat, as she deleted the message. "I'm finna go put this pussy on the nigga I shoulda been smashin' a long time ago," CiCi said, grabbing her bag and keys before walking out of the house. She hopped in her Audi TT, which she had custom-painted a plum color and put in her Beyoncé CD. She stopped by the nearest gas station to grab the Dutch Masters cigarillos for Boon. While at the counter, she told the clerk, "Lemme get a box; no, make that two boxes, of Trojan Magnums." She said it loud enough to be heard throughout the store. She didn't give half a shit about who heard it. CiCi paid for her items and got back in her car to head to Boon's spot.

Boon was anxious, to say the least, about his soon-to-be first, sexual encounter with CiCi. He had bought roses and loose rose petals from a local florist. Although they had been drinking earlier, he bought a brand new bottle of Louis XIII. The liquor ran through Boon, but he didn't care. He would spare no expense for the evening. He had lavender light bulbs in every light fixture in the house, as it was CiCi's favorite color. It was almost as though Boon had planned this night days in advance. He didn't have time to fix any fancy foods; besides, he had eaten earlier and wasn't hungry. He ordered CiCi's favorite Italian dish: chicken fettuccine, from a local take-out spot. It was set to be there in less than a half an hour.

Boon spread the rose petals from the doorway, to the dining room table, to his bedroom floor, and bed. He had a rose on the table, one on the bed, and one to give CiCi when she walked through the door. As Boon was in the bathroom spraying himself with Sean John's Unforgivable cologne, he heard his doorbell ring. He had on a lavender, Steve Harvey suit coat, white, Polo button-down, Polo denim, and some limited edition, lavender and grey Nike Air Force One's.

"I have a chicken fettuccine for D. Watson." The deliveryman was an acne-ridden teen, whose voice seemed to be going through puberty.

"That would be me. How much?" Boon asked, as he grabbed the food from the wiry-built young man.

The teen looked at the receipt and said, "$12.57, sir."

Boon handed the boy a fifty and told him to keep the change. The deliveryman was barely out of the driveway before his phone rang. It was CiCi.

"Yep?" he answered.

"I'm outside," CiCi said.

"Well, I'm waiting." Boon said, in high anticipation.

He ended the call and checked his appearance in the mirror once more. As he stepped out the bathroom, he turned on the light in the living room. The lavender flow dimly lit the couch and coffee table area. He grabbed the single rose off the dining room table, and at that very moment, his doorbell rang a second time.

Boon felt the slight perspiration on his palms, as his nerves were doing the Curly Shuffle, so he wiped them off on his jacket. He unlocked the door and turned the knob slowly, as if Chucky or some other killer was at his home.

"Hello, Daniel." CiCi said to Boon, shyly.

It almost seemed as though this was a blind date.

"Come on in, beautiful," Boon said, as he hugged CiCi when she entered.

The hug was a sensual one, full of pent up passion.

"Damn, you smell good as fuck! Look, even— "

Boon stopped CiCi in mid-sentence, pressing his lips against hers. She didn't resist. She slipped her tongue into his mouth, while he pulled her body passionately into his. After breaking away from the kiss, Boon locked eyes with CiCi. She was truly a welcomed sight and could pass for Gabrielle Union's identical twin. As she stepped past Boon, she was struck speechless. Lavender was her favorite color and its purplish tint illuminated Boon's spacious living room. Boon closed the front door, placed his hand on the small of her back, and led her to the dining room table. She noticed rose petals all over the floor and table and it almost brought her to tears. She thought she knew everything about

Boon, but his romantic side was a new thing for her.

"I know you haven't eaten, so I ordered your favorite Italian dish," Boon said, as CiCi sat her bag down and took a seat at the table.

"Oh my God, Daniel. I don't know what to say," replied CiCi.

Boon grabbed her food and a plate from the kitchen. The food was still piping hot, as he placed her plate in front of her. Once CiCi began to dig in, Boon fetched two glasses of ice and the two blunts he'd rolled for them while CiCi was out shopping. He then joined CiCi at the table and lit the L.

"You know, you got a strong-ass right hand on you, girl," Boon said, jokingly, while pouring them both a small glass of the costly liquor.

"I'm sorry, baby. I really wanted to power punch the li'l broad you be wit', but that ho whipped out on me." CiCi recalled.

Boon pulled long on the blunt, before sliding CiCi the glass and taking a swig of his glass himself.

"CiCi, I will be hard-pressed to find a gal that I love as much as I love you. I just wish you would've met me halfway long ago," Boon said earnestly.

CiCi was feeling her heart flutter. Boon was saying exactly what she'd been dreaming he would tell her.

"I got a surprise for you. Meet me in your room in 30 minutes and keep on everything you got on." CiCi couldn't hold out any longer.

She grabbed the blunt from Boon, her bag off the floor, and went to the bathroom to get ready. Boon was astonished. He had never sexed CiCi before, so to see her so straight to the point shook him. Nevertheless, he grabbed the liquor bottle, his glass, the other blunt, and headed for his room. He took the remaining rose petals and spread them all over the bed, before seating himself in his La-Z-Boy near the window.

"Close your eyes for a sec. No peeking either," CiCi said, when she opened the bathroom door. Boon smiled, but was obligated to follow her command. CiCi walked into the room and stepped past Boon, towards his radio. Boon could smell Love Spell by Victoria's Secret in her tailwind; CiCi knew it made him drunk with arousal. "Don't open 'em 'til I tell you to," CiCi said. She sat her iPod on the dock on his radio, and Ciara's "Body Party" began to play. "Look at me, Daniel," CiCi said, provocatively.

Boon opened his eyes and was dumbfounded. Before him stood an ebony goddess. His mouth was gaped open. CiCi stood before him in those fire engine red stilettos and the boy shorts and bra set she bought. She'd even donned the Mardi Gras mask for added effect.

"I only got one rule," CiCi began. "…no touching 'til the song's done."

Boon watched as she strutted towards him and began to slow wind in front of him. Boon took a big swallow of his drink. CiCi leaned over until her face was in his lap and whispered for Boon to unsnap her bra. When he did, she stood, still dancing and let the bra fall to the floor. Her 36D breasts were perky with their mocha-colored nipples. Boon reached into his pocket and pulled out $800 in 20's. When CiCi turned her back to him and made her ample ass bounce to the beat, he began dropping bills all over her body. CiCi sat in Boon's lap, grinding with her back against his chest. It was all Boon could do to keep his hands away from her.

"You want this pussy, Daddy?" CiCi asked Boon. She could feel his rock-hard dick through his jeans.

"Fuck yeah!" Boon responded.

"I'm lovin' that blazer. All that purple shit for me. I'm 'bout to fuck yo' head up, Boon."

CiCi murmured, as she bent over just as the song ended. Boon quickly leaned up and kissed her on her ass cheek.

"Don't move," Boon said, as he worked her boy shorts over her hips and down her thighs. When he looked up and became eye level with her pussy, he wasted no time tongue kissing her lips down there.

"Mmm… baby," CiCi moaned her pleasure. Boon lightly pushed her forward and CiCi put her hands on the floor. Boon palmed her ass cheeks, spread them, and commenced to burying his face in her juicy spot. "Oh fuck, Boon! That shit...feels...so good, baby." CiCi couldn't stop the orgasm.

Boon was turned on by her moans. He smacked her on the ass, as he continued to use his tongue to stimulate her womanhood. After making CiCi climax a second time, Boon stood up, took off his blazer, and began to unbutton his Polo shirt. CiCi turned around, still wearing the mask, and dropped to her knees. She unbuckled Boon's Ralph Lauren belt and unbuttoned his jeans. After carefully unzipping his pants, CiCi reached in and pulled out Boon's rod. Even though she'd seen it before, she was still caught off guard by the size. Boon was taking his tank top off when CiCi first took him into her mouth. She snaked her neck, as she bobbed into Boon. She took her hands off his tool, grabbed Boon by the thighs, and she began pulling him into her mouth.

"Fuck…mmm…hmmm…" Boon couldn't fight the moans.

He grabbed a handful of CiCi's hair, as she went to town on his wood. She moaned with every thrust and loved the way Boon fucked her mouth. Boon looked down and discovered her watching him with those bedroom eyes. He held back his climax and pushed her away from his stiffened love stick. CiCi lie back on the rose petal-covered floor and spread her legs. She grabbed a box of Magnums from her bag, just above her head, and handed it to Boon, who removed a condom.

"I want you so fuckin' bad," CiCi said, as Boon rolled the condom down over his penis.

He hovered over her and said, "Get that dick, girl."

CiCi didn't hesitate to grab Boon and guide him into her pleasure tunnel. On the way into her sugar walls, sparks seemed to fly immediately.

"Oh, baby," CiCi moaned, with ecstasy all in her tone.

Boon was still in push-up position, carefully feeling all of her depth. CiCi took a deep breath, as Boon pulled back to downstroke again.

"Take it all for me, CiCi. All of it," Boon said.

CiCi pulled her knees towards her chest and Boon began to long stroke her.

"Oh… yes… yes… yes. Fuck me, baby!" CiCi cried, aloud.

Boon was in heaven and continued his pleasant onslaught of CiCi's love. CiCi began to quiver, as she came on Boon's dick. She pulled him down on top of her, as she moaned louder and louder. Before she exploded again, CiCi rolled her and Boon over so that she was now the one on top.

"Ah, shit, CiCi. Ride that dick, girl. Bounce on it for me!" Boon commanded.

CiCi followed his instructions, immediately. She put her palms flat against Boon's chest and bounced on his dick, as if her pussy owned a pogo stick.

"Oh my God! Boon, you're the best, baby. Nobody can fuck this pussy like you. Nobody!" CiCi clawed into Boon's torso, but he didn't care. He felt that eruption coming. CiCi's walls contracted and was pulling the nut from his soul. "Daddy, I'm finna cum again!" CiCi screamed.

"I'm cummin' too, baby. Don't stop bouncing. Get it all fa me!" Boon demanded.

"Oh, shit!" They both screamed in unison.

CiCi's eyes rolled into the back of her head and Boon's body jerked, as his load caused his whole body to spasm. CiCi collapsed onto Boon's chest, exhausted, as if she had run laps.

"I want round two when I power up," CiCi said, between labored breaths.

Boon nodded in agreement.

CiCi had rolled off Boon to rest a minute. She went to the bathroom, grabbed her washrag and cleaned herself up. She picked up a clean cloth and wet it with warm, soapy water. She grabbed a towel and went back to the bed where Boon lay, slightly dozing off. CiCi washed Boon's flaccid penis with the warm rag. She dried it, threw the towels on the floor, and kissed up his thigh until she reached his pipe. She took his length in her mouth again and sucked him towards a fresh erection. Once Boon's tool reached maximum height, CiCi bent over and made Boon get behind her. Boon knew he wouldn't last long with all the ass CiCi was working with. He didn't grab a condom, and she didn't care; especially, once he slid into her and dug her out for the next 30 minutes. When Boon got ready to cum, he attempted to pull out, but

CiCi reached behind her, grabbed him by the rear and yelled, "Please don't stop! Oh fuck, I'm cummin' all on that dick!" Boon let go inside of her and fell over on the bed, spent.

CiCi curled up under him as they both nodded off to sleep.

At 2:45 a.m., CiCi was awakened by Boon's cellphone buzzing. She thought it was hers, until the lit screen displayed, **New Text Message From: Amerie**. CiCi instantly scowled at Boon's phone, but smiled devilishly. She looked back and saw that Boon was still out of it. She grabbed Boon's phone and opened the new message.

Amerie: Can you come put me to sleep, Daddy?

CiCi shook her head. *I got something for this bitch*, she thought. CiCi got Boon's phone and climbed on the bed next to him. She used his phone to take three pictures. One of her kissing Boon's manhood, one of Boon knocked out asleep, and another of her flipping the middle finger. She sent all three pictures to Amerie with a caption that read: **Boon: Payback! And bitch, he been sleep!**

THE TURN

The next morning, Boon woke up before CiCi and decided to reward her performance with breakfast in bed. He made his way to the bathroom to relieve himself. He washed his hands and face, and then brushed his teeth. Boon made steak and eggs with toast and hash browns. He poured them both a tall glass of orange juice, putting both plates and glasses on a wooden serving tray. As soon as he walked in the bedroom, CiCi was waking from her sleep.

"Breakfast in bed, excuse my French, for a bad bitch," Boon said, as he sat the tray on the bed next to CiCi.

He leaned in and kissed her lips, as she rubbed her eyes.

"Eww, boy, my breath stank. Don't kiss me yet," she said.

"I don't give a fuck. Gimme sugar, CiCi," Boon said.

Reluctantly, CiCi gave up the smooches. No man in CiCi's life had ever warranted this kind of gesture. She was taken aback at Boon's efforts to please her. Also, CiCi was just beginning to notice there were rose petals everywhere.

"Boy, you a fool wit' the lover boy shit. I like it though," CiCi said, as she took a sip of her juice.

After breakfast, CiCi asked Boon if she could take him out for dinner the next weekend. Boon marked the date in his personal calendar.

"So, will you come by again?" Boon asked CiCi, as she got dressed to leave.

He was beyond pleased with the night he'd had and daydreamed of reliving that night. CiCi paused at the recollection of the events that transpired. Boon had given her the greatest sex she had ever known.

"Of course I will. I believe your ass knew I would too," she replied, grinning from ear to ear.

CiCi walked to the front door, followed by Boon.

"I hate that you have to leave, but I understand you have to get ready for work tomorrow," Boon said, as CiCi turned to face him.

"Me too; but hey, at least you got to tap this ass - finally. Besides, we have a date Friday," replied CiCi.

Boon didn't notice the look of uncertainty in her eye, as he leaned in and shared a long, lover's kiss with her. CiCi's vagina began to throb at the way Boon's manly grip pulled her to him. The couple kissed, as though they wanted to get another round of sexual tension relieved. However, CiCi backed away first.

"I love you, Boon. Really, I do," she said.

"Call me later, or I'll call you, okay?" Boon was mentally faded but managed to say, "I love you too, Curelle. I'ma hit yo' line a li'l later, a'ight?"

CiCi smiled and Boon didn't close his door until she was in her Audi and driving off.

Boon went to his room and decided to play a couple of Xbox One games online. He and CiCi never smoked the other blunt he had rolled the night before, so Boon sat in his La-Z-Boy and lit his blunt. He grabbed his controller and sat back. Once he logged onto Xbox Live, it let him know that Amerie was signed in as well, because her gamer tag popped up. Boon was so captivated by his night with CiCi, he'd forgotten to call Amerie. He wondered what she was up to, so he sent her a message.

Boon: Aye. Feel like shooting it out?
Amerie: Check yo' phone, Daniel.

Amerie rarely called Boon by his first name, so it caught Boon off guard. Boon wondered what she sent to his phone. Maybe she called and he just missed it. Boon flicked the ashes off the end of the blunt and started playing Grand Theft Auto 5.

During gameplay, Amerie asked Boon if he had fun the night before. Boon thought about it and salivated at the sheer memories of the evening.

Boon: Why *you ask me that?*

Boon continued playing, until the next message came across the screen from Amerie.

Amerie: Still ain't check ya phone, huh? Boon, tame ya bitch before I tear into that broad. I don't play wit' li'l girls.

Boon was instantly panic-stricken, as if he had been caught with a kilo of heroin coming across customs. He paused his game and searched for his phone. After five minutes of searching, he found his phone in the pile of clothes he'd stripped out of the night before. Boon stared at the screen for a few moments, before mashing a button to illuminate the display. He had one, unread message from Amerie. When he went to the message, he was confused. It read:

Amerie: *I'm LMAO that you were here before me, but got yo' fix after me. Ain't it good though?*

Boon didn't understand what Amerie meant in the message, until he scrolled up and saw what alluded to this particular part of the conversation. Boon saw the pictures CiCi had taken in his phone. Under normal circumstances, he would've loved to revisit them often. This, however, was definitely not a normal circumstance.

"I don't fuckin' believe this girl!" Boon spat, aloud.

Just then, another text came through.

Amerie: I take it you got the message...just so u kno, I ain't trippin'. I knew she wuz gonna do it. She's catty. Me and u good. Hopefully better now.

Boon called Amerie instead of responding to the text. He was thoroughly flushed with embarrassment, but furious was an understatement of his sentiment towards CiCi. *How could she?*

"Hey, Big Daddy," Amerie said, when she answered on the second ring.

"Man, come on wit' all that. What the hell happened last night?" Boon asked.

He was glad to know Amerie didn't try to flip on him, but he was still 38-hot that the ladies had been using his phone to facilitate their dispute.

"Apparently, you got fucked and sucked to sleep last night. Too bad Ms. CiCi ain't wanna share," Amerie said with a chuckle.

"I got drunk, Amerie. I— " Boon began, but Amerie cut in.

"Boon, the wrong thing to do right now is to start lying. You been wanting to smash her for over a decade. I look at it like a milestone, really."

Boon only smirked. "I'm mad you know the history," he said.

"I pay attention. Honestly, I love you. You're not like any of the guys I've dated. If I had my way, I'd be wifey." Amerie hit Boon in the chest with this one.

He found himself pondering the thought of marriage. The past Boon had endured with women began to replay in his mind, including the pictures of him and CiCi. He didn't appreciate how she handled herself.

"I might need to take you up on that offer," he said, before giving it a second thought.

Amerie was taken aback.

"Are you trying me, Boon? Because, I'd white dress and bouquet shop today," she replied. Although she was laughing, she wasn't joking.

She and Boon had known each other a little less than a year, but had a plethora of things in common.

"You know what? Let's do that. I'm tired of dead-end women and you are someone I would love to hold onto," Boon said. "Lemme make plans for a dinner date at a restaurant and we'll rap about it further," he continued.

Amerie was all for it. "Okay," she said and hung up the phone, without giving Boon time to reply.

Boon took a deep breath. He was prepared to marry Amerie, but he was drawing blanks on how to break the news to CiCi, at least for a few moments. That was, until he realized how trifling she was the night before. He thought of Zo, Taz, Gia, Mela, and even Lil. Those women had crossed him the worst way. The mere memory of it all had him brimming with rage, to the point he didn't even realize that he'd dialed CiCi's phone. She answered on the first ring.

"Miss me already, huh?"

Boon wasn't the least bit amused. "What the fuck kind of games are you playing, Curelle?" Boon asked, with disdain evident in his tone.

CiCi knew exactly what he was referring to. "Daniel—"

154

"Daniel my ass, CiCi! I never thought *you*, of all people, would do some young-ass shit like that!" Boon was becoming more enraged as he yelled.

"Boon, that bitch tried me! How you gon' get mad at me for letting her know where I stand? She's new. I fuckin' been here!" CiCi hollered. Tears began running down her cheeks. She never thought Boon would take Amerie's side, if it came down to it.

"So, you comin' back had nothing to do with me? It was because 'that bitch tried' you, right?" Boon asked, rhetorically. "Sad it took for you to feel like you were in a race with someone for you to lay down with me. I woulda preferred for you to just keep cuffin' the pussy on me," Boon said solemnly.

"Boon, please...I...we just...not now. I wasn't trying to start nothing. I was jealous and— "

Boon was already content with his decision. "Jealousy is a wasted emotion. It just cost us something special. I don't want to see your name and number on my caller ID. Have a good one, CiCi." Before she could say another word, Boon ended the call.

CiCi was shocked. She sat on her couch and began to cry. She had just solidified her relationship with Boon; she knew it, but shot it down just as quick. She dialed his phone, but was sent to the voicemail.

"Boon, please talk to me. I know you're upset, baby, but please don't just turn me away like this," CiCi sobbed into the phone.

She called three times afterwards, but just gave up after that. Her heart was paining her. She had been in love with Boon for years and now he was gone. She went to her room to cry herself to sleep.

*

As Boon sat on his recliner, he exhaled and rolled a blunt, forgetting the one he'd already been smoking. After it was successfully rolled, he grabbed his laptop and made dinner reservations for him and Amerie at 9 p.m. He smoked his blunt, as he contemplated marriage to Amerie. She was fun, smart, self-employed, beautiful, and not to mention, she cut a fool in the sheets. He grinned, as he blew out a big cloud of weed smoke.

"I can do this. Hell, I wanna do this. Amerie, you got yaself a hubby," he said, as he puffed the blunt twice more and put it out. He got up and went to take a shower. Standing under the steaming water, he let it roll over his body from

156

head to toe. Not only did he have flashbacks of sex with CiCi, he also had pictures of sex with Amerie in his head. He thought of the messages CiCi sent to Amerie and fought back his anguish.

*

After showering, Boon dried off and sat naked on his bed. He grabbed his phone and called Amerie.

"Hello?" she answered.

"Hey. We're on for 9 p.m. I'll be at your place to grab you around 8:15," Boon said.

Amerie liked that he was assertive. It was a turn-on. "I'll be waiting," she replied.

Boon hung up his phone and threw it on the bed. He went to his closet to grab something to wear. After a 20-minute debate with himself, Boon decided to wear some tan-colored, Akoo, denim jeans, a red, blue, and tan Akoo button-down shirt, and his Akoo varsity coat, which was red with tan sleeves and blue patches. He even had the Akoo beanie. He got dressed and slid into his wheat Timberland boots. Boon looked and felt like a million dollars. He grabbed his car keys, his phone, and his wallet and headed for the door. Before walking out, he hit his body with Gucci Guilty cologne and gave himself the once-over. Satisfied with his appearance, Boon stepped out into the cold, Chicago afternoon.

*

Boon headed north towards the city and decided to call his brothers. Drakus was first.

"What up, youngin'?" Drakus said through the phone. He was happy to hear from his little brother.

"Same circus, different clowns, Drake. Check it though; I called you first, so I hope you feel some kinda way about that." Drakus was still silent. "You there, nigga?" Boon asked.

"Yeah. I'm just tryna guess what you gonna tell me. Knowin' you, some broad done did you the worst way, but I don't wanna assume the worst," Drakus said. Boon hated to hear that, but it had been commonplace for things like that to go on with him. "Wait, does it involve CiCi thick ass? Ah shit, youngin', you finally slapped bellies wit' her, didn't you? Drakus asked, excitedly.

"Naw, mu'fucka. Well, I finally smashed, but that ain't what I'm callin' for," Boon said.

"Damn, bro. Conquerin' that ass been a lifelong goal for you and you don't sound the least bit happy. Did it stank? No, wait, lemme guess. She don't suck dick?" Drakus guessed, covering all the bases. He was like an investigative reporter.

"Will you shut yo' face and let me talk, nigga? Damn, Drake!" Boon spat. "First of all, no it didn't stank, it smelled like water. Second of all, I believe that bish can suck the stripes off a Zebra. Not that it's any of your biz though."

Drakus was proud to hear his brother say those things. "So, you must got bad news then, 'cause nothin' could be better than that," Drakus assumed.

"I'm getting married, Drakus," Boon said. He was tired of his brother's rant about Curelle.

"To CiCi? Damn, she must've fucked and sucked you to death, nigga," Drakus laughed loudly on the other line.

"Man, you are an asshole, bruh. I'm marrying Amerie, Drake. I'll tell the family; don't you say shit," Boon warned.

"You talkin' 'bout the triplet with the ass and long, pretty-ass hair? Ohhhh... shit! Baby bro, you in there like booty hair!" Drakus said; he was proud of his brother.

"Drake, I gotta call Dooley and Deysha too. I'ma call you back," Boon said and hung up.

He didn't want to have a long conversation about his love life. Boon was glad he was riding in the car alone, because Drakus made him mad by talking about CiCi. Drakus would've loved to hear about the picture messages, but Boon thought it was ignorance at its best.

*

Boon walked into Jared's at 6:50 p.m. He was greeted by a female salesperson that instantly put him in the mind of Halle Berry in *Boomerang* - hairstyle and all.

"May I help you, sir?" the lady asked.

"Show me your engagement rings, please," Boon said.

"Right this way." The saleswoman turned and walked Boon to a glass case towards the back of the store. "Do you have a price range in mind, sir?"

Boon had not given it much thought, but he just shrugged his shoulders and said, "No more than $15,000."

The saleswoman's eyes lit up. She walked Boon closer to the register and slid the case open. She pulled out a tray of rings that glittered and glistened like little disco balls. Almost immediately, Boon saw one he liked.

"I want that one." He pointed to the white gold band with two, Princess-cut diamonds. One was black and one was white. The lady picked the ring up from the tray to give Boon the exact price.

"My apologies, sir. One of my associates must've placed this ring here. This one is actually a bit more expensive. It's listed at $22,350." The woman went to put it where it belonged and Boon stopped her in her tracks.

"Um, ma'am, I want it," Boon said and pulled out his AmEx Black Card.

"Shall I gift wrap it?" the saleswoman asked. Boon waved his hand in dismissal.

"Just make sure it's in a nice box," He answered.

"The boxes these pieces come in are customized, ivory boxes. The boxes alone are valued at $1,500 themselves." The lady said. As the saleswoman rang up Boon's ring, he pulled out his phone to call his other brother, Dooly. "Sir, the total is $24,361.50," she said, before swiping Boon's credit card.

"Bruh, lemme hit you in a few. I'm talkin' to the ex," Dooly said in Boon's ear.

"Okay," Boon said, taking his ring from the clerk and placing it in his pocket. He put his credit card in his wallet, smiled at the saleswoman, and walked out the store.

*

Boon hadn't realized he'd been in the jewelry store for 45 minutes and was going to have to rush to Amerie's house. For some reason, Valentine's Day in Chicago brought major traffic. Boon's phone rang, as he jumped on the expressway.

"Yo," Boon said.

"Bruh, what's up? Just returning your call," Donovan said on the other end.

"True. Um… I called to tell you I'm getting married, bruh," Boon said, and paused to hear Dooly's reaction.

"To who? CiCi, huh?" Donovan guessed.

"Hell no!" Boon didn't even want to hear that name anymore.

"I'm marrying Amerie, Dooly," Boon said.

"The girl with the sisters? From the homecoming party last year?" Dooly responded, with much enthusiasm.

"Yep," Boon said, proudly.

"Okay, then. I'm proud of that. Got you a good one, Boon. A good one," Dooly said.

"I'm tryna drive, so I'ma hit you later wit' more info. Don't tell Ma and Pops. Lemme do it," Boon instructed.

"Cool. Just hit me up, boy," Dooly said, just before hanging up.

*

Boon got to Amerie's house at exactly 8:00 p.m. He walked to the door and knocked three times.

"Who is it?" Amerie said from the other side of the door.

"King Ding-A-Ling," Boon joked.

"Fuckin' right you are," Amerie said, as she opened up. She stepped back to let Boon in and he kissed her lips, as he walked past. She had just gotten out of the shower and was still draped in a towel. "I'm getting dressed now, Papi. You lookin' good enough to fuck four times," she flirted, as she walked to her room.

"Is that a promise?" Boon asked, as he went to the kitchen to fix himself a glass of water.

"If you think it's a game, we can postpone this dinner date," Amerie said, with sincerity.

"Naw, baby, let's go eat first," Boon said.

Decent Proposal

Amerie stepped out of her bedroom, looking like Miss America. She was wearing an indigo, form-fitting dress made by Christian Dior. The dress had silver sequins on the sides, and her shoes were silver and indigo, Chanel, peep-toe heels. Her hair, lightly curled, hung down her back and shimmered with radiance. In her hand, she held a Chanel clutch that was silver with an indigo Chanel logo.

"Aw, shit. Can I taste you?" Boon said, flirtatiously.

Amerie smiled and struck a model-like pose. "You like?" she asked, batting her long eyelashes.

"Girl, you gon' make some women jealous tonight. You wearin' the hell outta that dress!" Boon exclaimed, as he walked around her, sizing her up.

The Paris Hilton perfume was intoxicating and Boon struggled to fight off his hormones.

"You ready?" Amerie asked, looking at her watch.

If they didn't leave right then, they would most likely not find another classy spot to dine for the evening. After all, it was Valentine's Day.

It was 8:52 p.m., when Boon pulled up to the exquisite eatery on N. Halstead Street, and as expected, it was already full. Love was in the air, as couples sat at their tables in the eloquently-decorated, five-star restaurant. Everyone was dressed in their best, and appearing to be wrapped up in their dates. Boon approached the hosts' podium just inside of the entrance. A blonde-haired, blue-eyed woman stepped up and welcomed them.

"Watson. Reservation for two," Boon said in his professional voice.

The woman looked at her reserved tables list in search of Boon's name. "Daniel Watson, table for two at 9 p.m.?" she asked for confirmation. Boon nodded his head. "Right this way." The hostess walked off to direct Boon and Amerie to their table.

Boon put his hand at the small of Amerie's back and followed both her and the hostess to their table.

Boon had reserved a table not far from the bar and equal distance from the kitchen. After being seated, Boon and Amerie's server for the night came to the table.

"Hello. My name is Vanessa and I'll be your server for the evening," she said, as she sat a bottle of Cristal on the table. Boon had pre-

165

ordered it when he'd reserved the table. "Would you guys like a few minutes to decide what to order?" Vanessa asked.

"Yes, please." Amerie said, as she turned off her cellphone. Boon followed suit. Tonight would have zero interruptions. "I love it in here," Amerie said, once Boon sat his phone down.

"You've been here before?" Boon asked, as he poured them both a glass of the expensive champagne.

"No, not ever. It's just overwhelming when you walk in," Amerie explained.

The soft, nude lipstick on her full lips had Boon's undivided attention.

"I feel the same way every time we're together, Amerie," Boon said.

All Amerie could do was blush. They both took swallows of the chilled Cristal.

Vanessa came back to the table to see if the couple was ready to place their order. After they had made their selections, Boon asked the server to show him where the restroom was. As they walked away, Amerie poured herself another glass of the tasty champagne. She admired Boon's swagger, as he walked with Vanessa.

"Oh, yeah. He is definitely a keeper," she said, aloud.

She hadn't given any more thought to the conversation about nuptials that her and Boon had earlier. She knew he was pissed. She was, however, thinking of how CiCi's face must look now. She got fucked, true enough, but Amerie was getting wined, dined, and later on, dicked out of her mind.

Ten minutes passed by and Boon was still not back at the table. Amerie was a bit fidgety and was about to excuse herself to the ladies' room just to not be abashed by sitting alone. Just as she began to slide out of the booth, Boon came back and reclaimed his seat across from her.

"Nice to see you didn't fall in," she said, sarcastically.

Boon laughed. "My apologies, sexy. Apparently, everyone had to use the restroom at the same time," Boon said. "So, Ms. Reynolds, if you could live in any other state, where would it be?" he asked.

Amerie sat back a bit and pondered the answer to his question. Not even 30 seconds after thinking on it, she said, "I guess I would have to say Texas." Boon was puzzled.

"Why Texas?" he asked.

"I dunno. I guess growing up in this cold-ass city has made me long for a warmer climate," she replied.

Boon, a Chi-Town native himself, understood perfectly.

Boon then locked eyes with her and took a knee. As he reached for her hand, Amerie's heart skipped a few beats.

"Amerie, since we met, you have been more than the often clichéd, breath of fresh air. You have not judged me, ridiculed me, and you were ready to do some gangsta shit when a broad set me up. I was always taught that God is the only perfect being. Well, today I have to disagree with that. You are perfect—perfect for me." Boon locked eyes with her, as he paused momentarily. Vanessa came to the table with a round, covered platter, and sat it in front of Amerie. Amerie had tears streaming down her face. "Before some gentleman tries to take you away from me, I want to know if we can share the rest of our lives together, so I can show you just how perfect we can be together." Boon took a piece of paper from his pocket and handed it to Amerie.

Hands trembling, Amerie opened it up and read: *Open the tray.*

Amerie turned and opened the tray. There sat the ivory, jewelry box, open and displaying the engagement ring.

"Amerie, will you marry me?" Boon asked, nervously, hoping she would accept.

"Oh my God, Boon. Yes! Yes! I will marry you, baby," Amerie exclaimed.

She was now crying, not solitary tears, but the waterworks. Boon grabbed the ivory box and took the ring out. He slid it onto Amerie's ring finger and leaned in to kiss her. As their lips locked, the entire restaurant was applauding them and their engagement. After the kiss, two other servers had come with two more platters, which actually had their food on them. Boon took his seat, as Amerie took a few napkins to dry her face. She was extremely overjoyed and trying her best to calm herself; but how could she, with the ice on her finger distracting her every thought?

"I have got to give it to you, Boon, you are very unpredictable. How the hell did you pull all of this off?"

Boon looked at the ring. "By simply wanting what is best for you." He answered. Amerie said nothing further. She and Boon were both famished and began to dig into their meals. "So,

Texas you say? What part?" Boon asked, referring to the question he'd asked her earlier.

"Wouldn't really matter. All of Texas is practically hot, but I know you like sports, so we gotta go where they have football, baseball, and basketball teams." Amerie said. "I mean, you were asking to see where we could move to, right?" she asked.

Boon nodded. He was glad he didn't have to ask, because he didn't want Amerie to think he was trying to move her away from her family.

Boon was stuffed. The porterhouse he'd ordered had him satisfied and Amerie was finishing off the last of her filet mignon. Compliments of the chef, came in the form of a cream cheese cake with cream cheese and caramel frosting, a light drizzle of fudge, shaved chocolate, and crushed almonds. The couple decided to take it to go. Boon flagged down Vanessa and asked for the check. When she returned with it, Boon didn't even look at it. He simply handed her his AmEx Black Card and a cash tip, totaling $150. Boon had already tipped the chef and the other servers involved in his proposal to Amerie. Boon stood and stretched his limbs, as did Amerie. Vanessa came back and handed Boon a receipt and his credit card, and thanked him and his new fiancée for choosing Alinea to get engaged. He smiled warmly and he and Amerie walked out of the establishment. Before exiting, Boon took a digital camera out of his inside jacket pocket and had the hostess take a few, random shots of him and Amerie.

"Please, tell me we can go home now," Amerie said.

"Damn, babe. Am I boring you?" Boon asked.

"Heavens no. Boy, please. I'm just beyond anxious to feel your skin on mine, baby. I need that," Amerie said.

Boon was almost instantly erect. "Okay. We goin' to Joliet?" Boon asked.

"Too far. My spot is less than 20 minutes away," Amerie said, as they climbed into the Challenger. Boon sat in the driver's seat and started the car. Amerie was tugging at his zipper. Boon leaned his seat back, as he backed out of the parking space. By the time he was on the road, Amerie's mouth was on his pipe. She bobbed up and down on it, until Boon pleaded with her to stop, so he could maintain control of the car. She looked at him, smiled, and said, "You better not kill us," before taking him back into her mouth. It was an erotic thrill, to say the least. She stayed *south* the entire 17-minute trip. Boon was ready to thrash her pussy.

"See how you ain't wanna let up? I'm finna tear that ass up," Boon said.

Amerie knew he meant it and it made her wetter to hear it.

*

The couple walked in the house, so caught up touching and fondling each other, they almost forgot to disarm the security system. She practically ran upstairs to meet Boon. He had taken his jacket off and was unbuttoning his shirt. She kicked out of her Chanel shoes and dropped to her knees. Boon's zipper was still undone, so she just took his button loose and pulled down his pants and boxers. She picked up where she left off in the car, attacking Boon's penis, hungrily, with her mouth.

"Mmmm," Boon moaned, as he dropped his shirt to the floor. He reached down and unzipped her dress for her.

"Come here," Boon growled.

Amerie stood up and turned her back to him. She felt Boon's rock-hard piece poking her, as she leaned her body into him. Boon helped her out of the $2000, Christian Dior dress and she let it fall to the floor. Boon leaned over, kissing her on the neck and shoulders, as he stepped out of his boots and pants legs. Amerie was aroused like never before. Boon unsnapped her bra and reached around her to cup her breasts. He lightly rubbed both nipples, before giving them both a little tug. Boon began kissing down her spine until he reached her panty line. She had on a pair of navy and white, pinstriped thongs. Boon eased them off her and kissed her crack. Amerie walked towards the bed and bent over it, placing her palms face down. Boon caught the hint. She was ready for him to deliver; not now, but right now. Boon stepped up behind her and gave her a preparatory slap on the ass.

"Yes, Daddy. Do it again," she said, huskily, and Boon obliged. He spread her cheeks and looked down at her pretty, glistening, wet womanhood, before slowly sticking his dick in. Amerie nearly stood up straight, as Boon's elongated hammer filled her insides. "Shit, Boon!" she yelled in pleasure.

"That's right. This is my pussy!" Boon began to dig Amerie out, as if he was looking for a new home in her vagina.

Amerie couldn't fight her urge to yell, as she threw it back. "Oh, yes. Oh...Oh...Oh...Fuck me!" Amerie was cumming already.

Her pussy muscles were gripping Boon's dick like the Jaws of Life. After Amerie's trembling subsided, Boon flipped her onto her back and drove the dick home once more. Amerie's legs were straight up, along Boon's torso; as he rhythmically stroked her, he would turn and kiss her feet.

"Damn, girl. This pussy is the fuckin' best, Amerie." Boon's face said it all, even if he hadn't. He pounded his way into ecstasy and Amerie loved every minute of it. When Boon felt his eruption formulating, he pulled out of her and shot his seeds across her stomach.

*

The couple lay next to each other, spent and out of breath.

"Damn, you got that Grade-A, USDA approved meat," Amerie told Boon.

"I take it that you're satisfied then, huh?" Boon asked.

"Very," she agreed.

She held her left hand up and they both looked at her ring.

"You like it?" Boon asked.

Amerie looked at him, as if he knew the answer to his own question.

"Baby, I love it. The only way this ring will leave my hand is if the finger is taken with it", Amerie shot back. "It looks like it cost you an arm and an ass cheek, though. Not trying to be intrusive or anything, but what'd it hit you for?" Amerie wondered, aloud.

"Not nearly as much as you're worth to me," Boon replied.

"I knew you would hit me with somethin' like that. Real shit though, how much?" Amerie asked again.

"Well, if you must know, I paid a little less than 25 grand for it," Boon said; to him, the amount was peanuts.

"Twenty-five thou', Boon? Why? I mean, don't get me wrong; I am in love with it. But I got a fuckin' Kia on my finger!" Amerie had a crazy smile on her face.

Boon laughed at her last statement. He hadn't thought of it that way, but it was true. It was all good though. He loved Amerie enough to do it for her again, if he needed to.

"Girl, you are worth every, red nickel too. We need to put the wedding together. Well, you can. I'm gonna out— "

Amerie interjected, "I don't wanna wait. Let's get married now and just have a big reception."

Boon wanted to have a small wedding, but didn't want Deysha to invite CiCi. He didn't want to see her again.

"Okay, so how do we tell your family?" Boon asked.

"My mom and dad actually recommended I marry you. You know my sisters have been asking whether or not I thought you'd propose," Amerie said with joy.

Boon felt good about the news. "Well, my brothers know and are happy for us. I gotta tell my parents, which should please them thoroughly. I'm the baby, and they have been waiting for me to get married," Boon said.

Amerie turned towards her fiancé. "I didn't hear you mention Deysha. When will you tell her?" asked Amerie.

Boon had an unsure look on his face. "I'ma tell her. I just hate how she have CiCi all up in my business, and this latest stunt CiCi pulled just got her a best friend short," commented Boon.

Amerie smiled and threw her leg over Boon. "You can handle that however you like, but for what it's worth, she's still your sister. I think you should tell her. After all, I ain't worried about CiCi. Not at all." Amerie sounded sure of herself.

"Okay," Boon began to rub Amerie's thighs. "So, we can take off work tomorrow and elope then?" Boon asked.

"Sounds good to me," Amerie said, as she flashed that million-dollar smile at Boon.

Amerie rolled over on top of Boon and began kissing him passionately. Boon felt the warmth from her love tunnel on his wood and it began to stiffen. They made love again, before passing out for the night.

Unreceptive

The 15th of February began as a beautiful, end of a winter day in Chicago. It was unusually warm for that time of year, but Boon and Amerie would be much appreciative of the warm weather. Amerie was in the bathroom showering and singing. The beauty of her voice awakened Boon. He joined her in the bathroom and climbed into the hot water with her.

"Well hello, handsome," she greeted.

Boon smiled and said, "G'mornin', gorgeous." Boon was tired and the shower was just what he needed to wake him up. He grabbed Amerie, whose back was facing him, and pulled her body to his. "You love me, right?" Boon asked.

Amerie turned around to look at him. After kissing his lips, she said, "Of course I do. You not gettin' cold feet, are you?" she asked Boon.

"Hell naw, ma. I'm gon' be real, though. I'm horrified of gettin' my feelings tampered wit' again; that's all," Boon said, as he began to lather his rag with Zest soap and wash himself.

"I share the same sentiment with you, in that aspect, Boon, but I show and prove. I am wit' you for who you are and how you love me. With your smarts, looks, affection, and swag, I aim to please from now until," Amerie said.

Boon smiled. "Spoken like a true boss," he murmured and Amerie was cheesing.

"How we dressin', Boon? Flashy or just throw something on?" Amerie asked, as she entered the enormous walk-in closet.

"I say we go sporty. I'ma put on my boy, Derrick Rose's Bulls jersey and a funky-ass pair of Jordan XI's with the red patent leather. I saw some all-black Versace pants in Macy's too." Boon had his outfit in mind.

"Well, damn! I guess I can rock my Walter Payton Bears jersey and my Son of Mars Jordan's. How 'bout that?" Amerie asked.

Boon nodded. "Oh, let's do it," Boon said, in his best Waka Flocka Flame voice.

Amerie laughed to herself, as they got dressed.

The couple met in the living room, looking like they were headed to a sporting event, rather than the Cook County Courthouse to get married.

"My car or yours?" Boon asked.

"Mine." Amerie grabbed her keys and stepped towards the door, with Boon following close behind.

Amerie started the car and put on Boon's
favorite Meek Mill song, "Ooh Kill 'Em."
That's how her and her fiancé felt right now.
They were on top of the world, and it showed in
their demeanor, as they drove towards the
courthouse.

*

Boon got out of the car first and went around
the Camaro to open the door for his bride-to-be.
She was glowing, as she stepped out the driver's
side of the American muscle car. Hand in hand,
they walked into the courthouse.

May I help you?" the receptionist asked, as
they approached her desk.

"We're here to tie the knot, ma'am. Where
do we go?" Boon asked.

The woman, with her dried-out Jheri curl,
was obviously having a bad hair day. Gruffly,
she said, "Do you both have ID?"

Boon and Amerie nodded in unison. The
woman gave them the directions to the place
where they would wed.

The words, **Family Court**, were engraved in
the plate on the door. Boon and Amerie pushed
through and went inside. There was a couple on
the way out and only two other couples seated

and waiting to be assisted. Behind the counter was four ladies, one of whom motioned for Boon and Amerie to step up to her.

"You two are here to get married, correct?" the Florida Evans look-alike asked.

"Yes, ma'am," Boon responded.

"Fill out these forms and bring them back up when you are done."

The woman slid a clipboard to both Boon and Amerie, with some questions they both needed to answer. They sat down and filled out the forms with their information.

By the time they'd finished, the other two couples had gone and it was 11:00. They handed the woman the forms and were given a single sheet with their information on it to give to the judge.

"The next available time is noon, in courtroom 6-B, on the sixth floor," said the lady behind the desk.

"Thank you," Boon said. Just before walking out into the lobby, he turned to the woman and asked, "Hey! Anybody ever tell you that you look like— "

The woman cut him off. "Esther Rolle. Do any of you wannabe comedians have any new material?"

Apparently, someone had beaten Boon to the punch.

"Come on, foolish." Amerie laughed, as she pulled Boon by his arm to follow her.

For the next 45 minutes, Boon watched, as Amerie passed Level 241 in Candy Crush on her phone. He was stuck looking at it, because on his phone, he was stuck on Level 180. Amerie was still glaring at the screen on her iPhone when Boon's cellphone rang. It was in his pocket and he fought to pull it out from the small, Versace pocket. He looked at the caller ID and saw Deysha's face.

Hesitantly, he answered. "Sis?" Boon said, drily.

"Damn, is that any way to answer to your big sister?" Deysha asked.

"I'm a li'l busy. What up though?" Boon asked.

Amerie looked up from her game and asked Boon who he was on the phone with. He showed her the screen on his phone.

"What you doin'?" she asked, as if it were any of her business.

"I'm getting married, sis," Boon said, matter-of-factly, and Amerie was smiling on the inside.

"You can't be serious. CiCi said she been tryna call—"

Boon didn't want his day ruined with conversations about Curelle, so he interrupted her. "Miss me wit' any of that CiCi bullshit. Anything else on the agenda, Mae?" Boon asked his older sibling.

After a slight pause on the phone, Deysha said, "No wedding, so there has to be a reception, right?"

Boon and Amerie hadn't planned a date for it, but Boon gave Deysha one anyway. "Yeah. March 14th," he said.

"Where at?" she asked.

"My house. Look, Mae, I gotta go. I'll call you later," Boon said and hung up the phone.

"You okay?" Amerie asked Boon, as they headed for the courtroom.

"Ready to be your husband; that's all," he replied and kissed her lips.

*

There was nothing extravagant about the actual ceremony. The judge gave the couples present the option of not having to hear the vows or actually hearing them. Either way, they were married and would receive their official marriage certificates in less than two weeks via U.S. mail. Boon and Amerie opted to receive

their nuptials, minus the vows. Boon sent a
message to his brothers and his sister, letting
them know that he had officially gotten married.
He even sent a message to his partner at his law
firm, Tayshun, and informed him as well.
Amerie was beaming with joy and it was
emanating off her.

"So, Mrs. Watson, how you wanna celebrate?
Have an old expensive bottle of champagne with
me?" Boon asked.

"Cool. Our first drink as a married couple,
Boon. What you got in mind?" Amerie asked.

She'd had expensive wine, but Boon was
something of a sommelier when it came down to
it.

"How about we grab some Aubry 'Sable'
Rosé?" Boon suggested.

"Never heard of it, but run it," Amerie
agreed, as they hopped into her car and peeled
off.

*

Three weeks had passed, and so far, marriage
was exactly what Boon and Amerie wanted it to
be. They had been so wrapped up in each other's
attention, they eventually forgot to put together

the wedding reception. While sitting on the couch playing NBA 2K14, Boon's phone rang.

"Hello?" Boon answered, without looking at the caller ID.

Amerie's Golden State Warriors were beating him by five points, with the time dwindling in the fourth quarter.

"Aye, you ain't givin' nobody info on the reception, nigga?" Drakus spat.

"My bad, boss. We been puttin' it together. Dress how you want, bring who and what you want." Boon was more interested in not losing to Amerie for a third, consecutive time. He put his phone on speaker and sat it on the table.

"Okay, but is the date and stuff still the same?" Drakus asked.

"Yep, bruh-in-law," Amerie said, as she dropped another three pointer with Steph Curry.

"What's up, Amerie?" greeted Drakus, not knowing he was on speakerphone. "Boon, Mae and Dooly on the phone too."

"Well, I guess I don't need to tell you to pass on the info. Look, I'll see y'all Saturday. I am getting my ass kicked over here," he said and hung up the phone.

"Boon, we got to get shit ready for the reception, baby," Amerie said.

She was excited to be Mrs. Watson and the reception was days away.

*

Saturday morning came and Amerie's sisters, Ashley and Alexis, came to help get the house ready for the guests. Boon, Drakus, Dooly, and their father were barbecuing, while their mom was in the kitchen making sides. Deysha still hadn't shown up.

"Daniel, I guess you got tired of slangin' that wacker every which-a-way, huh?" Daylon Watson, Boon's father, asked jokingly.

"Yeah, Pops. Amerie's just what I needed."

Daylon looked at Boon and said, "What happened to ol' CiCi? The dark-skinned honey with the two asses?" All the fellas, except for Boon, started laughing.

"She turned into the rest of the women I dated, Pop. Can we not talk about that today?" Boon said.

No one objected.

*

By 5:00 p.m., there were 15 tables set up and decorated in Boon's spacious backyard. Still, there was plenty of room for dancing, the badminton net, and horseshoes. There was even enough room for all the kids running around. Tayshun subbed as a DJ for the event. He was stationed on Boon's back deck, spinning a new mixtape from a new artist called Sinsay. The particular song was Sinsay's rendition of Kendrick Lamar's "Poetic Justice."

There were ribs, chicken, steaks, brisket, corn on the cob, potato salad, macaroni and cheese, collard greens, baked beans, hot dogs and burgers for the kids, coleslaw, and many other sides. For dessert, there were cakes, pies, candy apples, and all types of chips and cookies. All around the yard, you could find coolers with beer, soda, water, and juices in them.

The evening was starting out perfectly.

*

"Hubby, you good?" Amerie was walking towards Boon with two cups in her hand.

She was dressed in a pair of white, Robin's Jean shorts, a gold and white, Robin's Jean, fitted tank top and a pair of Robin sneakers. Her outfit was banging and the shoes alone cost an easy $600. She handed Boon one of the cups.

"Happy than a ma'fucka," Boon said.

He had on a pair of white, YSL, cargo shorts with a rose-colored YSL shirt. His belt and shoes were both rose-colored gator skin and both made by Maun. To say the married couple's attire was killing shit, was being modest.

"Lemme take a few pictures of y'all right now," the photographer said.

He was a friend of Dooly's and said he'd take photos for the whole reception. Amerie and Boon posed for several shots, as he snapped away. He took pictures of the in-laws, the food, the DJ, and more. If it was in the backyard, it was in a picture.

By 7:30 p.m., the backyard was crawling with guests. Boon's old classmates were there, old college professors, and the guys from his old basketball team. Amerie's family was huge, and it seemed that they all came to show their love and support. The music was pumping through the concert-style speakers, kids were running around playing, and the adults were conversing or engaging in one of the many activities going on. Amerie was mingling with her family members and Boon was talking with his brothers.

"Aye. I still haven't seen Mae," Boon said.

As if on cue, Dooly said, "Speak of the devil."

Boon and Drakus turned to see their sister walking into the backyard. When Boon turned to sit his drink down, he heard Drakus say, "Ah shit." His tone hinted that the shit was about to hit the proverbial fan. Boon whipped his head around to see what the "Ah shit" was for, and it didn't take long. Behind Deysha, was none other than CiCi.

That surprised Boon, indeed, but it paled in comparison to what he hoped his eyes had tricked him into seeing next. There were five other women tagging along behind CiCi, and Boon recognized every one of them. Behind CiCi was Lil, in a raunchy-looking romper and some sandals. She was tacky as hell, but at least her hair was done. Behind Lil was Gia, wearing a yellow sundress and yellow flip-flops. She wore her hair in micros, pulled back into a ponytail. Next in line was Zo, clad in a pair of navy blue Chuck Taylors, a denim, Citizens jean skirt that showed she was a white girl with ass, and a navy blue T-shirt with a picture of Marilyn Monroe on it. Mela, who had on a tie-dyed linen dress, trailed Zo and her hair was done in a Mohawk. The sight behind Mela made Boon cringe, and he became heated, instantly.

Taz was not only there, but that bitch was shining. One side of her head was shaved and

189

she had her nickname cut into it. The rest of her hair was left to hang and was dyed blonde with bronze streaks. She had on a Gucci halter top that was red and green, the red Gucci shorts to match, and a pair of white on red Stan Smith Adidas.

The group of women walked through the yard, as though they were performing artists the crowd had been waiting to see.

*

"What the fuck is this about, Deysha?" Boon asked. He was seething.

"You said bring whoever we wanted, so I brought what you passed up on. Don't worry, they were not for you."

Boon couldn't believe his ears. His own sister.

"Are you in…fuckin'…sane?" he shouted.

Luckily, the music was blasting and no one, other than the people next to him, could hear him.

"Boon, we just wanted to meet the lucky girl. That's all," Gia said, as she stepped forward.

Amerie and her sisters saw Boon, his brothers, and the crowd of women holding their attention.

"Can you guys come with me for a second?" Amerie said to her sisters and walked towards Boon and the uninvited guests. "Boon, is everything okay? Hey, Deysha." Amerie stepped next to her husband and spoke to her sister-in-law.

Boon took a deep breath. Amerie's eyes met with Deysha's, and immediately, Amerie could tell that she was up to some bullshit.

"Babe, this...these...um," Boon didn't know what to say and Lil was not ready to be standing much longer.

"Honey, we all ex-girlfriends," Lil said.

"I know, Lil. Nice to meet you," Amerie said and reached her hand out for a shake. The exes were awed and Lil shook her hand. "Gia, right?" Amerie greeted Gia the same. "Mela, sorry we didn't get acquainted at the hospital, but I'm Amerie." Amerie was surprising the shit out of Boon. She continued her intros. "You must be Zo, and Taz, of course." She shook Zo's hand and Taz's a bit firmer. When she got to CiCi, she said, "Glad you could make it, Curelle." CiCi rolled her eyes. "Deysha, we have plenty to eat and drink. Make yourselves at home." Amerie used her left hand to pull a lock of hair behind her ear, making sure the exes' eyes, along with Deysha's, focused on her engagement and wedding rings. "Baby, you ready to eat?" Amerie asked Boon, as she grabbed his arm.

"Yeah, let's go smash the groceries," Boon said, still feeling unsettled.

He walked away with his wife and his sisters-in-law and left his brothers with the exes and his trifling-ass sister.

*

The night went by smoothly, after the ex-girlfriend club meeting, and everyone seemed to be enjoying themselves. Boon's mom, Laurie, sat and talked with Amerie's mom, Ava, about their families. The fathers of the married couple were drinking and talking about the old school music groups. Boon's exes were at a table, not far from the table of gifts. The DJ turned the music down, as Boon and Amerie addressed their guests.

"Good evening, everybody," Boon began. "First of all, we would like to thank everyone for coming out to celebrate with us." The crowd applauded.

"Daniel and I are looking forward to our future together and realize how lucky we are to have all of your support," Amerie added, looking at the ex-girlfriends' table.

"I hate that ho!" CiCi said, to no one in particular. She was still salty about Amerie drawing down on her a few weeks ago. "Wait 'til she comes this way. I bet I slap that bitch. Boon knows he dead-ass wrong for this shit," she said.

"Not if I jump on that tramp first. Like somebody give a fuck about her sisters and shit," Zo piped in.

"So, lemme get this straight; y'all 'bout to beat this broad up because she married a nigga y'all had, but can't have?" Gia said.

She wasn't over Boon either, but she didn't want to look like a groupie.

"Don't act prissy, ho. Boon told me 'bout your li'l hot ass," CiCi said, looking right at Gia.

"All y'all played my boy out. At least show him you better than this goody-goody he got now," Deysha chastised them, walking to the table.

Her relationship with her husband was rocky lately and she was in her *misery loves company phase*.

"I'ma pop it off. He knows I'm wit' the fuckery," Taz said.

She wanted Amerie's spot as well. She'd sucked and fucked her share of ballers, but not one had taken her seriously. Boon was as close as she'd come. The other women at the table, she would have bowed to gracefully, but not this new bird.

*

Boon and Amerie had wrapped up their thank yous and made their way towards the gift table to open their gifts in front of their guests. Taz and the other exes stood from their seats. Deysha sat down. As Boon and Amerie passed by the exes, Taz yelled, "Bitch, you ain't nobody!"

When Amerie turned towards the comment, Taz was in the middle of swinging a right hook. It caught Amerie in the jaw, followed by a left cross that sent her staggering backwards. Boon snatched Taz up from behind, but couldn't stop Zo, Mela, Gia, and Lil from attacking. Ashley and Alexis hurried to aid their sister. Taz turned in Boon's grip and said, "Boon, please. I deserve you, not this—"

Boon reached back to a happy place with his right hand and swung forward with great force, slapping Taz down to the grass. She lay there, holding her face and withering in pain. When

Boon looked towards the fight, he saw that Amerie was fighting Zo and Lil, CiCi was boxing-out Ashley, Alexis and Gia were on the ground tussling, and Mela was now backing away with a bloodied nose. Somebody had socked her square in her snot box.

"Aye, man, y'all wanna help me break this shit up!" Boon yelled to his brothers. He went and pushed Lil to the ground. Amerie was mounted on top of Zo, giving her the business. "Babe, chill. It's over!" Drakus grabbed CiCi and Dooley was holding Gia. "I can't believe y'all came and turned my shit out like this! I knew y'all was some scandalous women, but this is low!" Boon glared venomously at each ex. Taz was picking herself up off the ground. "Zo, Gia, Mela, and Lil, this is my *wife*, Mrs. Watson. Respect that and leave my house. Now!" Boon yelled. "Taz, I should call the law on your conniving-ass. Get the fuck away from my crib, before I slap you wit' my other hand. And CiCi, just when I thought I was wrong for not inviting my *best friend*…" There was no mistaking the sarcasm in his voice when he addressed CiCi. "Thanks for coming. I don't need to see you again, *friend*!" he said.

"Boon, why you actin' like that?" Deysha asked her younger brother.

"Deysha, I would love to call you many names right now, but out of respect for the lovely couple that gave us life, I just want you to leave; and take the ho patrol you brought with you." Boon and Amerie walked into the house.

All of the guests had gone, except for Amerie's sisters and parents, and Boon's parents. Boon was tending to a knot on Amerie's cheekbone, when the remaining guests came to join them in the living room.

"Son, I like how you handled yourself today, but don't be slappin' these hoes. Let Amerie do it," Amerie's dad said, and the entire room laughed. "On the real though, we're headed home. We love you two; take care of my daughter," he said.

"I will and thanks again for coming." Boon shook hands with his father-in-law and hugged his mother-in-law.

"Sis, we brought the gifts inside and the backyard is cleaned up. Y'all be good; and Boon, keep them scallywags away from my sister," Alexis said, half-jokingly.

The group hugged and then went out the door. Boon's mother pulled Amerie away from Boon to talk in private for a second, and let Daylon have a moment with his son.

"Son, you got a good, strong woman there. Keep an eye on her though, ya hear?" he said to Boon. His dad had never steered him wrong, so he only nodded. "Me and ya momma got Deysha, don't worry," Daylon added.

Boon's mom hugged him and told him she loved him, as she and Daylon said their goodbyes and left.

So, I guess we're alone now." Amerie said, removing her gold shirt.

"Yes," Boon said, as he started to undress as well.

Amerie kissed him on the lips and pushed him down on the couch. She straddled his lap and began kissing him again.

"What's our next move, Papa Bear?" Amerie asked Boon, taking a brief intermission from the kisses.

"I take it you mean –after - I deliver this dick. Truthfully, we packin' and movin' to Texas," Boon said, before he turned off the light and made love to his wife and her war wounds.

Happily Never After

Four months after the reception, Boon and Amerie found themselves living in Houston, in a lavish, four-bedroom mini-mansion, with a two-car garage on each side of the home. They were only 20 minutes from Reliant Stadium, where the Houston Texans played its home football games. Being that both were from a big metropolis area, it was comforting for the couple to live and work in a big city. They opened up a law firm together, Watson and Watson, in the Downtown Houston area.

It was the week after Independence Day and the sweltering heat was unlike any other heat Boon or Amerie had known.

"This damn sun gotta nigga sweatin' like a hooker in church," Boon said, climbing out of his new, triple black Chevrolet Tahoe.

He was dressed in a pair of white, linen shorts, white, linen Polo, and a pair of Mauri gators that were all white as well. Amerie hopped from the passenger side of the truck and rounded it to join her husband. She was laughing, tickled by Boon's last statement. She wore a lime green, Ralph Lauren, summer dress and a pair of white Jimmy Choo sandals.

The couple was out to grocery shop for the dinner they had planned for the night. Boon had just won his first case in Texas and they wanted to celebrate it. Although they had been in H-Town for only four months, they didn't have a hard time making friends. Boon had begun working out at a local gym four times a week, and became acquainted with two guys there, Barry Shields and Julius Glover.

Barry was 5'7, wiry thin, dark-skinned, and bald. He was a real estate agent, married for the last six years, and a father of three. He told Boon his friends called him "Slab". That's what the natives called Cadillacs, Barry's only car of choice.

Julius, or "J.G.", as he was known, was taller than both Boon and Slab. He stood 6'4 and was about 235 pounds of mostly muscle. He wore a low fade with deep waves, had a peanut butter complexion and was tattooed from wrist to shoulder on both arms, and all over his torso.

"What are we going to cook, baby?" Amerie asked Boon, as they entered H-E-B grocery store.

"I guess we can whip up a huge pan of lasagna, corn on the cob, and some garlic cheese toast," Boon said.

"I know you and the guys are gonna be on y'all beer shit, but me and the girls are gon' sip on us some Moscato and a couple wine coolers." Amerie said.

She was referring to Slab's wife, Tiffani, better known as Tip, and J.G.'s wife, London, whose nickname was Lola. The three ladies had grown close and spent a great deal of time together.

"That's cool. Let's make it quick, if we can. I'm tryna get out this heat," Boon complained.

On the way back home to Harris County, Boon's phone rang, as Amerie drove. The number that showed up in Boon's caller ID was a strange number with a 704 area code. It wasn't peculiar for potential clients to call Boon from random numbers, so he answered. "Hello, this is Daniel Watson," he said with his professional tone.

"Boon, we need to talk," the woman on the other line said.

Boon now recognized the area code as belonging to North Carolina and Gia was the only chick he knew from there. However, the woman on the line sounded nothing like her.

"Who is this?" Boon asked, reluctantly; he actually wanted to hang up.

"Who you think this is?" the woman asked back, and Boon caught on to the voice, finally.

"Look, scandalous, find another nigga's line to play on," Boon spat and hung up.

"You okay, baby?" Amerie asked, as she turned the SUV into the subdivision.

Boon wiped his hand over his face and gazed out of the window.

"Amerie, I told you that I wanted to change my number and I should have. That was CiCi, for the 12th time in almost as many days," Boon said, revealing the identity of the caller.

Amerie was shaking her head.

"You must've fucked the life outta that girl. It don't bother me, babe. I mean, if that's why you were gonna change it," commented Amerie.

Boon thought about the night before Valentine's Day. He did drill CiCi real good.

"Fuck it; I'm changin' the number when we get in the crib," Boon said.

Amerie didn't object.

Once in the house, Boon powered his phone off. CiCi had called four more times after he'd hung up on her. They went to the kitchen and began cooking. Amerie went to their large stereo system and turned on Sinsay's "Kush Junkie." It was another song off the mixtape that Boon loved.

"Glad you turned that on, baby. As a matter-of-fact, can you twist one for me?" Boon asked over the music.

Amerie's phone was vibrating in her pocket. As she went to get the weed, she picked it up.

"State ya business," she said.

"Yo, we 'bout 15 minutes away," the heavy voice came through the phone.

Amerie pulled the cellphone away from her ear to check the caller ID. It said "Lola", but there was a man on the line. "J.G.?" Amerie asked, to see if it was Lola's husband.

"Yeah. I called Boon's phone a couple of times, but got the voicemail each time," J.G. explained.

Amerie secretly found J.G. attractive, but she loved Boon with her whole heart. She would never act on the attraction.

"Why didn't you just tell…wait…where's Lola?" Amerie inquired.

"In the store. Why? Somethin' you need to say?" J.G. asked, in a smooth tone.

"Are you expectin' me to say something, J.G.?" Amerie grabbed the weed out of her nightstand drawer.

"Maybe."

"I'll tell Boon y'all on the way." Amerie hung up.

She didn't know of J.G.'s intentions, or if he even had any, but she didn't want Boon to, remotely, suspect anything.

*

Boon and the guys sat in front of the 72-inch, plasma, Smart TV, playing Call of Duty: Ghosts. Amerie and the ladies were in the library looking at videos on WorldStarHipHop's website.

"Hey, Amerie," Tip called out, as she was passing Amerie the blunt. "What made you and Boon move down here from Chicago?" she asked.

Amerie took the blunt and hit it twice.

"The short version is, it's cold there, and Boon's ex chicks wouldn't stop wit' the stalker shit. Hell, one of them broads called his phone like 10 times today," Amerie said.

"I would've had to beat one of them hoes up before I left. Ain't lyin'," spat Lola.

She was from Chicago as well, but had been in Houston for the last seven years.

"Man, them hoes tried to jump on me at my reception. It was complete mayhem in that muthafucka!" Amerie recalled. Before either of the other women commented, Amerie saw a video clip she wanted to see. It was about a black family doing the wife-swap thing.

"Could either of y'all see yourself doing this shit?" Tip asked, as she watched.

"I be needin' J.G. to get another wife sometimes. That nigga sex drive is too high. I swear he be eatin' off them inmate trays at his job." Lola and the girls laughed.

Julius was a detention officer at Harris County Jail and could dick Lola down every single night if she let him. For some inexplicable reason, this moistened Amerie's panties. She was daydreaming about his muscular, tattooed arms hoisting her up and sitting her on his wood.

"Hell naw. Slab gives me enough problems. I damn sho' don't want to deal with another nigga's issues," Tip spat. "What about you, Amerie?" Tip asked, but got no reply. Amerie was still in La-la land.

"Amerie!" Lola yelled, a bit louder, and snapped her out of her trance.

"My bad. I was thinkin' 'bout my session from last night," Amerie lied.

She hit the blunt and passed it back to Tip, without answering the question. She didn't bother passing to Lola, because she didn't smoke.

The couples ate, drank, laughed, and even sat and watched *The Hangover Part III*. It had gotten rather late and they decided to call it a night. Everyone said their goodbyes and were preparing to leave. Just before leaving, J.G. asked if he could take a plate home.

"No problem. Babe, can you fix it for him? I got to let loose. Damn beer is runnin' through a nigga," Boon said and raced to the toilet to take a whiz.

Lola went to wait in the car. Amerie was in the kitchen fixing the plate, when J.G. walked in.

"Call my job tomorrow. Ask for me. I know you know the number; and I saw you watching me at dinner. I won't tell if you won't," he said, still keeping a safe distance.

Amerie wrapped his plate and handed it to him. She looked in his eyes and stammered, "G… goodnight, J.G."

She felt awkward, but it made her tingle. Deep down, her promiscuity was fighting to surface. She knew she would call him. Backing away, J.G. knew she would too.

The next afternoon, Boon was at the office, waiting on a client. Amerie had gone home to prepare dinner for the two of them. As she stood by the refrigerator, she had a flashback of J.G.'s words to her: *I won't tell if you won't*, he had told her. Amerie was a closet thrill-seeker and the unattainable was always something she sought after. Hesitantly, she lifted the phone's receiver and punched in the 10 digits.

"Harris County Jail, this is Officer Friday."

"I need to speak to Sergeant Glover, please," Amerie said, uncertain of why she was attempting to disguise her voice. Moments later, he answered the line.

"Sergeant Glover speaking," J.G. said.

"So, I called. Now what?" Amerie asked.

She was being a fox and it was turning her on with every passing moment.

"Now, you say when. I say where. We be grown about this shit, when we get there." J.G.'s straightforwardness was doing numbers on Amerie's libido.

"Okay. How's Friday?" Amerie asked.

"Sounds good. What you gon' tell Boon?" J.G. quizzed.

"Wrong answer. You should be telling me where, not concerning yourself with Boon," Amerie spat back. She wanted to level the playing field.

"Okay, feisty. Marriot in the City then. Paying for room, as we speak," J.G. said.

"How I know what room?" Amerie asked.

J.G. laughed a little. "Pick up a key in your name. I'll leave it at the front desk. No matter what time you get there, I'll be ready," J.G. said.

"I'ma be there at 9 p.m. sharp," Amerie said and hung up.

*

The week seemed to breeze by. A couple workdays here, a few date nights there, and soon, it was Friday. Boon loved to go and watch the high school football games, which was very popular in Texas. Amerie didn't go with him to many of them; she used that as her *me* time. Tonight, she was planning to share her *me* time with J.G.

It was summer, so the schools were only scrimmaging, but Boon decided to go anyway. He dressed and kissed Amerie goodbye, as he left at 7:45 - exactly the same time he always left. Amerie waited until she saw the yellow Porsche Carrera head up the street, before she got dressed herself. Just in case Boon beat her home, she dressed conservatively. She wore a pair of Levi cargo shorts and an Oscar the Grouch tee. She put on her green Chuck Taylor Converse and made her way to the Marriott.

When Amerie got to the hotel, it was only 8:30. Therefore, she went to the bar, located inside, to have a drink. She ordered two shots of Grey Goose, paid for them, and drank them quickly. By then, it was 8:51, and not only did she no longer have cold feet, but her entire body was warm. She was horny and feeling devilish.

She walked up to the front desk and gave the front desk attendant her ID.

"There should be a key here for me," Amerie said.

The clerk gave her the card and told her, "Room 618." Amerie went to the elevator.

Before getting on, she texted Boon.

Amerie: Went to get a drink or two. C u later. Luv u.

Boon: *Okay. Luv u 2. B safe.*

Amerie made it to room 618 and didn't hesitate to the open the door. When she walked in, she could hear the shower running.

"J.G.?" she called.

"I thought you would renege on me," he called from the bathroom.

Amerie took the time to check the room for other occupants.

"Naw. We grown, right?" she replied.

"True," J.G. said, as the running water in the shower ceased. Amerie was tipsy, so she sat down on the king-sized bed and kicked off her shoes. The bathroom door opened and J.G. emerged. To Amerie's surprise, he was completely naked. That wasn't all she noticed.

He was well-hung and it made her salivate. His entire upper body was tatted and rippled with muscles. He walked towards her, while using his right hand to stroke his dick. Amerie couldn't fight her inner freak anymore. She leaned forward and took J.G.'s length into her mouth.

"Mmmm… " J.G. threw his head back in satisfaction. Lola had him on pussy rations and he was backed up. He couldn't wait any longer. "Lemme get those shorts, girl," he growled at Amerie.

She plopped his erection out of her mouth and turned her back to J.G. He aggressively pulled down her shorts and green thong. Amerie began rubbing her clit, as she bent over. J.G. put on a condom and went up in her. His penis wasn't bigger than Boon's, but he handled her as if she was light as a feather and she loved it.

"Oh, shit! Oh, J.G! Fuck me!" she yelled. "Damn, this dick feels so good!" she moaned.

*

Before the sex was done, J.G. used his phone to record some of the action, convincing Amerie that he'd use it to masturbate to when Lola wouldn't fuck him. Amerie was still tipsy and had endured a good vaginal pampering, so it didn't take long to convince her.

By 10:30, Amerie was pulling into her own driveway to get in her own bed. She hoped Boon wasn't horny, because J.G. had just rearranged her insides. Luckily, Boon wasn't home yet. She jumped in the shower and then went to bed. Twenty minutes later, Boon was home and curled up next to her, dozing off himself.

*

Seven months later, Boon and Amerie had been living and loving the married life. Boon's uncertainty had vanished completely. Amerie was a godsend. They were sitting down watching *Maury* together. The episode featured cheating women and their lie detector tests.

"I'm glad that part of my life is over. I started really feeling the urge to bash one of them hoes' heads," Boon said, recalling his exes.

"Babe, you know how I kick shit. All woman, no slut," Amerie lied.

In fact, she and J.G. had fucked at least 30 times. She would have failed a lie detector test miserably.

"That's why I put a ring on it," Boon said, kissing Amerie's lips.

He got up to go roll a blunt and Amerie checked her phone, as a text message came through. It was from Lola.

Lola: You lucky I ain't comin' back 'til next week. But you betta be ready.

Amerie was lost and texted back.

Amerie: Wut u talkin' 'bout?

In less than two minutes, a multimedia message was coming through. Amerie opened it and dropped her wine cooler. 'Oh, yes. Fuck, yes, Daddy!' came loudly from her speaker. Boon heard it and thought she was watching porn on her phone.

"Damn, baby, lemme see that," he said, licking the blunt closed, as he ran back into the living room.

"Boy, please; that was a ringtone I'm 'bout to use for your calls."

Boon smiled and took out his lighter. Amerie was frantically trying to think of what to do. Boon's phone rang while another text came through to Amerie's phone. Boon went to the bedroom to get his phone and Amerie opened the text from Lola.

Lola: And since I know u ain't gon' show ya hubby, I just sent it 2 his phone myself.

When Amerie looked up, Boon was already watching the video.

"Boon—" Amerie began, but Boon cut her off.

"Oh, you know you can shut the fuck up talking to me!" he spat. "You a dirty bitch! How fuckin' dare you?" he asked, rhetorically.

He began to feel *that* rush. That urge to bash in her brains, and the thoughts of all his exes crept into his mind. Only this time, he actually married the bitch that scarred him. In his mind, Boon could see them all laughing at him. To add insult to injury, he could see Deysha laughing too.

At that moment, Boon wasn't the same anymore; he'd snapped. He was smiling, but on the inside, something devilish was going on. All he could think of was how he was going to murder his exes, including the newest member of them all—Amerie.

*

"I need to go and see my mom," Boon said, with a major attitude. He went to his closet and began packing a suitcase.

"So, what about us and here? Can I come?" Amerie asked.

She genuinely regretted her promiscuous behavior, but the damage had been done.

"We good. I'll be back in two weeks. No— I don't want to see you. Besides, you and J.G. got a lot to talk about, it seems," Boon said.

He seemed to be dealing with what was going on well, but he was a ticking time bomb. Boon finished packing, went to his truck, and threw in the suitcase.

"Boon, can we at least talk about this before you just up and leave?" Amerie pleaded.

Boon looked at his wife and shook his head. "I'll be back in two weeks. If you still here, we gon' talk then."

Boon pulled out of the driveway, headed to Chicago.

A Lil Issue

Boon made the trip back to his hometown in what seemed like a flash. In actuality, it took him 11 hours to get to his mom's house in North Chicago. He had driven the entire way without resting, stopping only twice for gas and to take a leak. He could feel his body twitching, impulsively, as the video of Amerie replayed in his mind. His mind then switched to his first heartbreak. He remembered how he wanted to make her pay for her shattering his heart.

Boon got out of the truck and went inside. He and his siblings all had keys to their parents' house. He got there at sunrise and let himself in. To his surprise, both his mom and dad were up, drinking coffee in the living room.

"Son, why haven't you been answering your phone?" Daylon asked his son. "I called you twice and your mother has been calling, constantly, and worried sick," he continued.

Boon's mom was walking toward him with a disturbed look on her face.

"Daniel, your wife called us around 5:30 yesterday and said you stormed out on her, and was headed here," Raven Watson explained to her youngest child. "She said you didn't tell her why or anything. Quite naturally, your father and I began to call you and began to panic when you didn't pick up for either of us," she said.

She hugged Boon tightly and he hugged her back.

"Ma, I'm good. Just needed to breathe a minute and see some old friends," Boon said to his mom, as they broke the embrace.

"Now, don't go lettin' yo' dick get you in any more shit, Boon. Your wife really cares about you, boy," Daylon said.

It turned up Boon's flame. She had everyone fooled, but not him - not anymore. Phase one of *Ex Out the Exes* was about to begin.

"Well, I'm here for two weeks. Y'all can handle 'ol Boon for that long, right?" Boon asked, before going upstairs to his old room.

That same afternoon, after getting a couple hours of sleep, Boon took a shower and got dressed. His mom and dad were gone, but he knew they would be back soon. The Bulls game was coming on and Daylon never missed a game. Boon hadn't eaten, but was content to grab some fast food while out. He got in his Tahoe and headed towards Hyde Park. He was on a mission to locate Lil. He didn't hate her worse, but he did hate her first. He had heard from old teammates that she lived in Hyde Park with her cousin, Fatty. Boon didn't have a plan;

all he had was a .357 Magnum and a chip on his shoulder.

When he pulled into the neighborhood, the block was jumping with gang activity and drug deals. Boon put his revolver in his LRG jacket pocket and walked into the store on the corner. He bought a big bag of Funyuns, a pack of bubble gum, and a 20-ounce Pepsi. Before he turned away from the counter, he heard someone say, "Boon, is that you?" He turned, slightly startled by the woman's voice. It was his old secretary, MaKayla Gordon.

"Kayla, what it is?" Boon greeted the heavy woman.

She was all but 50 pounds heavier now, but she was still a pretty, big girl.

"Shit. You quite a star. Mad clients been wanting your business. Some chick that you used to mess with came by the office looking for you," MaKayla said.

This, if nothing else, caught Boon's attention.

"What'd she say her name was?" Boon asked.

"I can do you one better. She left a name and address, but it's at the office. Call me in the morning and I can have all that for you," Kayla assured him.

Boon was antsy, but he didn't want her being too nosy.

"You remember what she looked like?" Boon asked, as he and Kayla walked out of the store.

"She was short. Real short and ghettoooo. Ooh, that broad was ghetto. She was dark brown and she had a nice shape too. I'll give her that. I think her name was Erica, or Essence, or some shit like that." Kayla guessed at the name. Boon still pretended to be baffled, although he knew it was Lil.

"Okay. Cool. I'ma call you in the morning, Kayla," Boon said, walking to the driver's side of his truck.

"Okay, Daniel," Kayla called out to him, "Nice seeing you again."

Boon nodded and got in the truck. Almost as soon as he got in and closed the door, the orgy Lil had with the football team, while they were together, ran through his brain and ran his blood hot. He shook his head, feverishly, and burned rubber off the block.

As Boon sped away from 83rd Street and Kenwood, his mind was still doing numbers on him. He wasn't himself anymore, but he didn't care. Something in him burst when he saw Amerie on the video and he saw blood.

217

Boon's cellphone rang and calmed him slightly. He hadn't realized he was doing 85 in a 45 mph zone. He slowed the SUV down within the speed limit and calmly answered the phone.

"Yeah?" he said, not recognizing the number.

"Um… I was looking for Attorney Daniel Watson," the man said.

"Speaking. My apologies; someone has been playing on my phone. How may I help you?" Boon made a valiant attempt to suppress his anger.

"I heard you were the best at what you do and I wanted to secure your services for my son," the man said.

"I'm in Chicago for the next two weeks, so I'm not certain what kind of time you are working with," Boon replied.

"He's out on bond now and his court date has been set to three months from now. I can wait two weeks," the man said.

Boon told the gentleman that he was driving and would contact him when he was stationary. After getting the man's name, Boon hung up.

*

Boon was in Grant Park, smoking a cigarette and taking a breather. In his brief moments of sanity, he wondered if he was tripping, coming out to Chicago to murder these women. However, his moments of lucidity were incomparable to his fury, when the thoughts of his exes' infidelity invaded his mental space.

His phone rang again, showing yet another unknown number.

"Daniel Watson," he answered with a clipped tone.

"You must want to talk. No number change. Then, I hear you're back up here. Why won't you at least have a conversation with me, Boon?" CiCi asked.

She sounded like she was going to cry, but Boon didn't give a fuck. Not even a little.

"You just as triflin' as the rest of them. Stop callin' me!" he ordered and hung up the phone.

For extra measure, he turned off his phone and wondered how the hell CiCi knew he was back in Chicago. *Mae and her big damn mouth,* he thought, fuming.

Boon had planned to kill CiCi too, but she was higher up on the totem pole. She meant a great deal to him, so she would be amongst the last to go. Boon was in his truck, headed back to his parents' house. He had gotten hungry, so he stopped and got McDonald's and continued to the house. By 8:00, he was in his room, watching the Knicks and Pacers basketball game. There was a knock on his bedroom door.

"Who dat?"

"Dooly, bruh." Boon unlocked and opened his door for his oldest brother. "Man, light this and politic wit' me." Dooly said, handing Boon a blunt.

"What up?" Boon asked, as he lit and hit the weed.

"Why you ain't let a nigga know you was here, bruh?" Dooly asked. "Better yet, why you ain't tell us you was movin' to fuckin' Texas?" Dooley was clearly upset.

"Aye! I don't wanna talk about that shit right now, my nigga," Boon said, sternly.

"Boy, I'm yo—"

"I don't give a fuck about none of that! I said, I don't owe you or nobody else no explanation about what the hell I do!" Boon yelled.

Normally, Dooly would've knocked Boon's ass all the way out, but something in Boon's tone made him decide against it.

"Okay, my nigga, let's just chill and burn. I missed you, li'l bruh. That's all," Dooly said, calmly.

The two men smoked and watched the game in an awkward silence. Dooly had hoped to have a sincere talk with his youngest sibling, but the look in Boon's eyes earlier, let him know to give him some space.

"Well, bruh, I'm 'bout to be out. I got a hot-ass date tonight. You know how it goes," Dooly said, standing from the desk chair he had been sitting in.

Boon only nodded and stood to shake Dooly's hand. Dooly was beginning to worry about Boon, but he decided to let it go for another time. Dooly left; Boon locked the door and laid back on his bed. He took out his phone and turned it back on. Once it had fully powered up, it showed that he had three text messages and two voicemails. He checked Lola's message first.

Lola: U owe me some dick. When u get back in Houston, call me.

The message actually gave Boon mixed emotions. On one hand, he wanted to get back at J.G., but on the other hand, Lola was coming off just the same as Amerie.

The other two messages were from the man he'd spoken with earlier about his son being a client. He left his name and number in one message, and the next message stated the best time frame in which to call. Boon then checked his voicemails. Amerie's voice was the first he heard; and against his better judgement, he listened to it in its entirety.

*

By the time the two minute and twelve second message was over, Boon was ready to drive back to Houston and kill her right then, although she was last on the list. The crying, and all the pleading she was doing, only reminded him of her moaning from J.G.'s strokes. She even went as far as to come clean about the fact that she was just an extremely promiscuous chick. Ideal case of too little too late. Boon erased the message and damn near threw the phone into the wall. Then, he realized there was one more voicemail he hadn't listened to. This one was from Kayla.

"Hey, Boon. I thought you had changed your number, but I see that you didn't. Anyway, I had to swing by the office to get a file for Tayshaun, so I grabbed that info for you. The chicks name is Ebony Charles and her phone number is 773-555-1217...." Kayla continued. Lil had left the Hyde Park address where she was living. When Boon thought about where the address was, he realized how close he had been earlier that day.

He wrote down the information and decided he'd call her early the next morning.

*

Boon lay down to get some type of sleep that night, but he tossed and turned. In fact, he got up at 5:00 in the morning, and left his mom and dad's house at 6:00 - before the sun came up. He was not far from the 75th and Lawrence address Lil had left him. He'd stopped by a 24-hour drugstore, near the old, Cabrini Green housing projects to buy a prepaid phone, before he got there. When he was close, he used it to call Lil.

"Hello?" a hungover Lil answered with attitude.

"I heard you was looking for me," Boon said, smoothly.

His mind was running away with him, but he needed to get through this smoothly.

"Boon?" Lil questioned, sounding more awake now.

"Yeah," he said.

"You in Chi-Town? 'Cause if so, I just want one last time. I know you married now, but I owe it to you. I haven't had sex in eight months, hoping you'd give me at least that much," Lil said solemnly.

Now you wanna be good to me, Boon
thought.

"I'm two blocks away. You alone?" Boon
asked.

Lil got excited. "Yeah. Hell yes. My cousin
is gone 'til next week sometime. You know the
apartment number, right?" she asked.

"Yeah. I'ma be there in less than 10. Be
ready for me," Boon said, making sure he had
loaded the .357.

"The door is unlocked for you, too," Lil said,
and they ended the call.

Boon got out of his truck, at a parking lot two
blocks from Lil's house, and walked to her front
door. He didn't want anyone to see his truck pull
away from her building. When he got to her unit,
he still knocked, as he turned the knob to enter.

"I'm in here, Boon," he heard Lil call from a
back bedroom. When he walked in, she was
laying naked on her back, rubbing herself with a
vibrator. "I figured this is what you meant by be
ready," she said, looking at Boon, as she
continued to please herself.

Boon's .357 was in the back pocket of his
jeans. He began to take his jacket off.

"Bend over, lemme see that pussy from the
back," he told her.

When Lil got on all fours, the image immediately reminded Boon of the position he'd seen her in when he caught her getting ran-through by the entire football team. Amerie's video came to mind; and before he knew it, he zoned out. He grabbed two of Lil's pillows, and as he mashed them against the back of her head, he put the revolver against them.

POW!

A single shot rang out, and Lil's hips fell so that now she was flat against the bed. Her head had burst under the pillows, on both sides, and brain matter was everywhere. As Boon came to his senses, all he could hear was the constant buzzing from her vibrator. Boon zipped up his jacket and left the apartment. The sun was almost over the horizon, when he got back to his truck. He turned on Meek Mill's "Ooh Kill 'Em", as he left Hyde Park.

Yo' Fault

As Boon headed Downtown to scout his next target, he had no type of ill feelings or remorse for blowing Lil's brains across her bedroom. He actually wanted to do it again. The rush from squeezing the trigger of the cold steel was orgasmic. Boon powered on his personal phone and dialed his voicemail. Once he got to Kayla's message with Lil's info, he deleted the message and hung up.

Boon had fallen asleep in his truck, in the parking lot of his old residence. He had set his phone's alarm for 8:30 and it was now going off, doing its job. Boon sat up and wiped his eyes. He didn't have any information on Mela's last whereabouts, so he decided to camp out at his ex-friend, Yo's house. Boon had last seen Mela at his wedding reception; but prior to that, he recalled seeing her at the hospital with Yo. From where he'd parked, he had a clear view of Yo's '96 SS Impala. Mela used to leave Boon's house for work at 9:15. And this morning, he was hoping she was at Yo's spot and kept the same schedule.

Just as Boon had been hoping, Mela came out of the building. However, she was with a little boy. Although Boon was psyched-out, seeing the boy with Mela made Boon spare her life - for the time being. As Mela walked to Yo's car, Boon's mind fuzzed for a minute and then cleared, just as the old TV channels did when you had to reposition the antenna. He was flashing back to the day he walked into Yo's apartment, and saw him in the act of beating Mela's pussy like a prizefighter. From that thought, his mind went to her stealing his money, and then the way she and Yo fronted at the hospital, as if they weren't the backstabbing scum that they were. It was all Boon could do not to grab the .357 off his waistband and kill Mela in front of her son.

Boon looked on, as the Impala drove off into the City. Boon got out the truck and made his way towards the building. He had no idea why, but he wanted to kill Yo as well; maybe because Yo took part in Mela's harlotry. In addition, Yo had also pretended to be Boon's friend. With these facts in mind, Boon ascended the stairs, instead of taking the elevator. Once he got to the floor Yo lived on, he checked his gun and saw that he had five rounds left. He knew Yo kept several guns, so he decided to go in using his brain, instead of brawn. He tucked his weapon in his belt, covered it with his shirt, and walked to Yo's door. Déjà vu hit Boon, instantly, as he stood there. He could feel his blood boiling; but instead if imploding, Boon simply knocked on the door. He could hear someone walking towards the door inside the apartment. The walking stopped and Boon assumed the owner of these footsteps was looking out the peephole. Boon didn't move a muscle. He looked directly at the lens of the peephole.

"Oh, shit!" the man's voice exclaimed. Soon thereafter, the locks began to click and Boon heard the doorknob turn.

When the door opened, Boon was face-to-face with Yo, once again.

"My bad for just dropping by like this. I'm in town for a few days and I just wanted to get some bud, my nigga," Boon lied.

Yo acted as if he'd never crossed Boon. Either he'd forgotten or he didn't give a fuck.

"You know you good here, boy," Yo said. "Come in. I was just about to light up and fuck wit' the game for a minute." Boon walked in and felt awkward. He wanted to shoot Yo right then, but the gunshot would be too loud. "Have a seat, homie. Grab a controller and get on this boxing wit' me," Yo said, as he lit the L and sat on the couch.

Boon sat down too, but told Yo he would rather watch him play the game. Yo hit the blunt and passed it to Boon.

"So, I see you been up on that new nigga, Sinsay," Boon said, making small talk.

"Yeah. That nigga nice as fuck. He from the ATL, but the nigga got bars like one of them BK niggas," Yo said.

Boon pulled the blunt again and passed it to Yo. Boon was glad Yo hadn't tried to bring up Mela, because he probably would've shot him then and just said fuck the noise.

After two hours of spectating, Boon gave in and played the game with Yo. It was now 11:50 and Yo got up to put on his favorite song, "Kush Junkie", off Sinsay's mixtape. Boon liked the song too; but right now, the loud-ass music punched his fuckin' button. The day he had caught Yo with Mela in the act, it was due, in part, to Yo's loud-ass music. Boon's brain had him envisioning that day all over again, and again. Everything seemed to get silent. Boon couldn't hear a thing, although the music was banging and Yo was rapping along.

Boon pulled the .357 off his waist and Yo turned to face him.

Boom!

Boon blew Yo's dick smooth off. Yo instantly dropped to the floor, screaming and pleading. "Oh, shit. Oh, fuck, Boon! What the fuck!" he spat in agony.

Boon heard nothing. He was in a crazed state of mind and wasn't quite done yet. Boon pulled his gloves out of his pocket and went to Yo's bedroom. Yo was a diehard Cubs fan and had a trophy case full of autographed memorabilia. Boon pushed over the trophy case, breaking the glass and scattering the items about. He then took out the autographed Sammy Sosa, Louisville Slugger, and returned to the living room.

Yo had managed to crawl towards the kitchen, but only four feet from where Boon left him. Boon saw Yo's mouth agape, but all was still silent in his ears. Boon went back, took Yo's blanket from his bed and placed it over himself like a poncho. He got three grocery bags out of Yo's kitchen and tied two of them around his shoes to make sure he didn't leave any shoe prints in the blood. He took the third, packed an outfit from Yo's closet in it, and brought it into the living room. Yo was motionless and in shock. He had lost a lot of blood and was moments away from dying. Boon was oblivious to Yo's current state, not that he would've given a damn. He stepped over Yo's body to place the bag of clothes by the entertainment center. Boon turned to Yo, but by this time, Yo was dead. Both his hands were placed where his penis used to be.

*

Hours had gone by and Boon was still in Yo's living room. The sounds of reality had returned to him, as Sinsay's "Kush Junkie" repeated for the umpteenth time. It was now eight o'clock in the evening, and Boon cut all the lights off. The light switch on the wall turned on the light in the living room, so he took the bulb out. Mela was a sneak, so Boon decided to rearrange the letters and be a snake. He sat in the dark, with only the loud music in his ears. He had been in the darkness for so long, his eyes had adjusted to the lack of light, and he could see everything. As he sat there, he remembered *that* day, again. The day Mela had left him.

She was the bitch Yo was on the phone with when they were at Boon's crib playing the game. Yo was laughing at him about only having one bitch, knowing all the while he was about to fuck his friend's girl. She turned away from the best Boon had to give, and for what? *For this*

231

piece of shit? Boon thought, as he peered at Yo's lifeless body.

Mela's sex faces in Yo's mirror began to dance around in Boon's mind. He couldn't fight them off. He wasn't sure he even wanted to. He was hurt when she left him, but pain was a part of life. Boon felt blatantly disrespected, when Yo and Mela hooked up. It was more than a slap in the face.

Boon stood from his seat and grabbed the Louisville Slugger. The speakers blared in Boon's ears. His thoughts were amplified in his mind. He could hear himself loud and clear. *That nigga told me to just walk in*, he thought. *Boy, they wanted me to walk in and catch them fuckin'; they had to.* Boon's thoughts were running away with him. He remembered how Mela had looked directly into his eyes the morning after, when she had slid under his covers and gave him head. She was Jezebel in the fucking flesh.

Boon's lid blew off. At this point, he couldn't even hear himself thinking. The silence had returned. There was no music, no thoughts, just silence and a yearning for brutal violence. Boon's head whipped around to give him a view of the locks, as they were turning, one by one. Still clad in the poncho and bags on his shoes,

Boon moved to position himself behind the door when it opened. He had his right hand gripping the bat and it was propped on his shoulder, as if he was on deck to be next in the batter's box.

The door opened and Mela slowly stepped in. She was flipping the switch on the wall, but it did nothing. She stepped in and closed the door. Boon saw her and his eyes damn near killed her with the look they had in them.

Mela was pissed. She hated when Yo had the music up loud. She had been trying to call him for hours to tell him their son was staying with her mom for the night. Unfortunately, while she was calling him, he was busy grabbing for the remnants of what used to be his penis. Mela stepped towards the entertainment system to turn off the radio, fussing as she moved through the living room.

Boon snapped— again.

If not for the loud music, Mela would have heard the plastic bags on Boon's feet creeping up behind her. He gripped the bat with two hands and gave the best "Hammerin'" Hank Aaron swing his arms could muster. His arm was perfect, as the bat cut through the air and collided with the side of Mela's cranium. Her head burst like a cantaloupe dropped from a high-rise window. She crumpled to the floor and just lay there, twitching.

Boon, still deaf to all noise around him, watched as she spasmed and blood pooled around her head. Boon wished he could stand her up and bash her head in repeatedly. Instead, he chose to step over her and grab the bag of clothes from beside the entertainment center.

Boon took the blanket off and dropped it in Yo's bedroom. He returned the bulb to the living room fixture and turned it on. He went to the bathroom and changed into the pants and shirt he had taken from Yo's closet. He put his clothes in the bag and tied it up. Boon was careful not to touch anything else, as he sat still and let some time pass. He wanted to leave in the wee hours, so no one would see him leave Yo's apartment.

At two o'clock in the morning, Boon had grown a bit impatient, and felt it was okay to leave. He had turned Yo's music down at 11 p.m., so the neighbors wouldn't call the police. Although the neighbors knew Yo played his music loud, Boon didn't chance it. He crept out the building and to his truck. He would scout again tomorrow.

"I'm comin', Gia," he said in his rearview mirror, as he headed to his parents' house.

*

Boon lay sprawled across his bed, knocked out in a deep sleep. He was dreaming about his Home Run Derby on Mela's dome and his Billy-the-Kid-type shooting, straight to Yo's dick. The brutal images playing in Boon's head would have been nightmarish to any other individual, but for him, it was more soothing than anything was. His heart had been tormented by this worthless duo. He was asleep, but he smiled in his brief slumber. Although his body lay still, resting, his mind had been hyperactive since he stood before Amerie in Houston, watching her adulterous performance on his phone. Mentally, he had been putting in overtime for three, consecutive days now.

At 10:32 am, a knock on his bedroom door awakened Boon. He rolled over, groaning at the time on his digital clock, sitting on his nightstand, beside his bed. The knock came again, louder this time.

"I'm coming!" Boon's voice sounded throaty from cottonmouth and morning breath. He swung the door open and was face-to-face with his dad.

"Come have a bite to eat with us, son. You been here two days and ain't really said much of nothing to me and ya momma," Daylon said.

Boon stretched and yawned. "Okay, Pop. Let me brush and wash and I'll be right down," Boon told his father. Boon's father was a great dad and had always had a great rapport with all four of his children. His bond with Boon was special, though. He always felt Boon was a pushover, at least until he couldn't take it anymore. Boon's brothers used to poke fun at him and Boon just ate it up. He wouldn't cry, get angry, or fight back. He would just isolate himself and shutdown. Daylon used to call Boon, "Balloon", because after a while of taking every joke and prank he could take, Boon would snap. He chased Dooly and Drakus with sticks, threw rocks at them, and fought with them until they finally just beat him up. On one occasion, Boon got so upset that he had pushed Dooly down the steps, causing Dooly to break his arm in three places. That was the last time Dooly tried Boon. He always said Boon had hell in his eyes, when he looked back up at him, standing at the top of the stairs.

Boon took a shower and brushed his pearly whites, before joining his father at the dining room table.

"Ya momma went to help ya Aunt Liz with some damn event she's catering, so it's just us two," Daylon said, as Boon took a seat at the table. His dad had made hash browns, country-fried ham, grits, eggs, and toast. Boon bowed his head and blessed his plate. After he finished, his dad shook a little salt over his food, before asking Boon, "How's married life, son?"

Boon's brain activated the mini sex tape Amerie had made, and he felt his temperature gauge climbing. "It's cool, Pop," he lied. "Why you ask?"

"Just making conversation, Daniel. You still a dynamite stick, boy. Shit gets better when you get old and grey. Trust me," Daylon said, with a slight chuckle.

Boon looked confused. "How you figure it's better when you old and grey? I don't get it," Boon quizzed.

"See, ya trying to find something in the fine print, Boon. Simply put, shit gets better, because you stop giving a fuck," Daylon said, as he and Boon laughed a hearty, stomach-tightening laugh. Little did he know, Boon had stopped giving a fuck about three and a half days ago.

Boon enjoyed the meal with his dad and the conversation as well. He sat down on his bed and turned on his cellphone. He took the clothes he had pilfered from Yo's house and placed them in a plastic bag. His phone fully powered on, and to Boon's surprise, he had no messages. As he took the bagged garments out, went downstairs and out the door, he decided to log into his Facebook account. Boon hit the unlock button on his remote to his truck, grabbed the bag off the backseat with his clothes from last night in it, and the prepaid phone from the cup holder. It was now 12:45 p.m. and Boon was heading to the backyard with both bags of clothing and the prepaid cellphone.

It was the end of winter, but it was still a bit chilly outside. Boon walked to the back of the house, heading towards an iron barrel his father used for his mini bonfires. He emptied the clothes from the bags into the barrel and then tossed the prepaid phone in there with them. He looked at his cellphone to scan his list of friends, as he went to his dad's barbecue grill to get the lighter fluid. Boon wasn't on Facebook for entertainment purposes; he was doing homework. When he got back to the barrel, he opened the lighter fluid and doused the contents in the barrel with it. He used more than half the bottle before setting it on the ground, a safe distance away from the drum. Boon pulled out his lighter and a dollar bill from his pocket. He lit the bill on fire and dropped it into the pile of clothing. Instantly, the flame blazed sky-high. As the fire crackled and burned, Boon continued to scroll through his Facebook friends list until he came to a particular status - Gia's. It read, "*At our fav spot. Missing him, but I still came.*" If Boon's memory served him right, their favorite place was not far from Lake Michigan. Of course, he assumed she was talking about him.

Before he knew it, Boon was in his truck, heading for the lake. He and Gia used to kick it there sometimes, smoking weed and watching the sunset. It was only two o'clock and way too early for the sun to be setting, but Boon was ready to take this proverbial shot in the dark. It was his only lead, and didn't have him involving anyone else. Before pulling in to a space on the roadside near the lake, Boon had stopped to get two roses for Gia - if she was there. He didn't want to frighten her by just popping up on her as if he was a stalker.

Boon looked around for Gia for a few minutes, inhaling the crisp, cold air blowing in off the water. He thought he was crazy for coming out there, not knowing for sure whether she was out there or not.

"Tell me if I'm dreaming. I must be," Boon heard, from a woman behind him, sitting on a boulder about 20 yards to his left. She was wearing a pair of baggy jogging pants and a Chicago White Sox leather coat. She was also smoking a blunt. As she got closer, Boon realized it was, indeed, Gia.

"Oh, please, tell me you're here to enjoy the sunset with me or a blunt? A conversation or something," Giovanni said, with high hopes.

Boon had to force a smile to his face, as he handed her the roses.

"These are for me?" Gia was genuinely surprised. The last time she saw Boon, he was a mad nigga, kicking her and his other exes out of his wedding reception. "What got you bringing me flowers, Boon?" Gia asked, as she passed him the blunt. Boon looked into her eyes for a moment, and then walked towards the boulder she was sitting on. Gia followed, closely behind. "I mean, thank you, baby, but why?" she asked, after Boon sat down.

He looked at her and said, "For the old's, the new."

Gia didn't understand what that meant, but she didn't want Boon to want to leave, so she sat beside him and just stared at the water.

Boon didn't realize he had been out there with Gia for three hours, smoking and talking. He didn't care. He wanted to kill her; and the more she talked, the more comfortable she would be to go wherever he suggested. "So where ya man at?" Boon asked, as Gia pulled on her skully, noticing the temperature had dropped since they'd been out there talking.

"Somewhere hoping you don't miss me like I miss you," she answered seriously.

That's what the fuck you get, Boon thought. Instead, he said, "You talk too much for me to miss you. If we linked up, you would make sure somebody knew, and I would hate for my wife to know. She still hates y'all for ruining our reception, too," Boon lied.

"I wouldn't tell nobody shit, Boon. I just want to be held and talked to all night, like you used to do. We are both adults. What I need to tell my business for?" Gia claimed.

It was music to Boon's ears. "So you want to get a room? You know I don't live in the Chi no mo'," Boon said, standing up to stretch his legs.

"Boy, please, I got a house now. A bitch doin' it big now," Gia said, laughing.

Boon shook his head. "Okay, doin' it big. I'm riding with you, then," Boon said.

"So you gonna leave your car here?" Gia asked, as they headed towards her car.

"I caught a cab here," Boon lied, again. "I mean, you said we pulling an all-nighter, right?" he asked.

Gia smiled, but didn't comment, as they walked to her powder blue Jeep Grand Cherokee and got in.

Gia had the heat on, so they both were warming up on the ride to her house. Boon noticed they were heading towards South Chicago. "Aye… can you stop us by a drugstore or a Walmart?" he asked. Gia pulled into a drugstore, as soon as she came up on one. Boon hurried in and bought himself another prepaid phone, some gum, and a soda. Before walking out of the store, Boon took the phone from its packaging and stuck it in his pants pocket. He got to the car and climbed back in. Gia thought he was stopping to buy condoms, but saw the gum and soda through his bag. She was on her period, so they couldn't have sex anyway. She wasn't menstruating heavily, but to her, it was gross to have intercourse while on the rag. However, she loved Boon though, so if he wanted her to, she didn't mind orally pleasing him.

Soon, Boon and Gia stepped into her small, three-bedroom house. It seemed spacious on the inside and proved to be so, when Gia told Boon she had a finished basement and an attic as well.

"Make yourself at home, Boon. I'm about to cook. You hungry?"

"Nah, I just got the munchies like a motherfucker. I don't know why my black ass didn't buy any junk food," Boon said, as his high was coming down.

"I got plenty of shit in the pantry. Help yaself," Gia said, as she clanged the pots and pans, in search of the one she was looking for.

Boon and Gia were seated on her love seat in the living room, watching *Harlem Nights* on DVD. The movie was close to the end, when Gia laid her head in Boon's lap. Within seconds, Boon had a full erection and Gia could feel it through his pants. At first, she paid it no attention, until Boon made it jump.

"Okay, okay, Big Daddy," Gia said, playfully. She looked at Boon and said, "I'm about to take a bubble bath. You mind coming in the bathroom to keep me company?"

Boon had feigned enjoyment the entire evening and couldn't figure out how to off this bitch. He needed to figure something out. "Yeah. Gon' and get ya underwear right. I'll be in there when you hit the water."

Gia kissed Boon's dick through his pants, making his dick throb, before going into the bathroom and starting her bathwater.

Boon could hear the radio loud and clear from the countertop in her bathroom. Lil Wayne's "No Worries" was playing. Boon laughed because, ironically, Gia really did have a worry. Boon was going to kill her. Tonight. He fought with his hormones and lost. His erection had been a stubborn one, as he walked into the steamy bathroom, with his dick still hard. Gia sat back in the tub, soaking, enjoying her bathwater with her eyes closed. Boon had rolled a blunt before going in. He stepped out to light it and came back in. Gia's eyes were still closed. Boon's dick was still hard. Boon used his lighter to light a candle that sat behind the stereo and turned off the light. Boon hit the blunt two times and blew out the smoke. Gia, smelling the cannabis, opened her eyes to the dimness of the bathroom and the strong aroma of Kush. Seeing Boon posted by the radio made her pussy jump and she wanted him. She reached out for her towel to dry her hand, as Boon passed her the blunt. Boon looked into her CD player on her small countertop radio. Drake's "Crew Love" was in it. Boon turned it on and put it on repeat. Gia passed him the blunt back. Boon turned the stereo down a bit. "You look good as shit, sitting in the tub full of bubbles," he told her.

"Nah, that's you. You got all buff, standing over me blowin' Kush, dick all hard and shit," Gia shot back.

Boon had to admit to himself, he wanted to bust a nut badly. "You always had that effect on a nigga, G. For real," Boon said honestly.

"I mean, you make it hard for a bitch not to put it on you. You packing," Gia chuckled, as she turned on the hot water to heat up her cooling bathwater some.

Boon and Gia finished smoking the blunt, after she turned off the water, and continued their conversation.

"Come here, Boon," Gia said, sitting up in the tub, as Boon told her stories about Texas. He inched towards her and had to step over the radio's cord to get to her. When he did, she pulled down Boon's sweats and briefs and his pole poked out, pointing at her like one of those Uncle Sam posters. She licked the mushroom head, as if it was a caramel-covered ice cream cone, and then took it into her mouth. She grabbed Boon's ass cheeks and force-fed the dick to herself.

"Mmmm… yes, Gia. Show out fa me. Be a bad girl," Boon groaned, seductively, as Gia sucked him sloppily from the seated position in her tub. She stroked Boon with every bob and moaned as she slurped. She took her mouth off as she jacked Boon's load down her shin and breasts. Boon was satisfied, for the moment.

Gia bathed herself, after talking for another five minutes about random stuff. The mood changed when she said, "Fuck that nigga, Shyne. I got my nigga, Boon, in here."

Boon's mind immediately went back to his sole purpose for even being in Gia's house. Murder. The name Shyne brought back another *fucked-up-bitch moment* in his life. As The Weekend sang his part on "Crew Love", Boon's mind replayed the pornographic phone call he listened to, as Gia, his then girlfriend, was screwing Shyne's brains out.

Suddenly, the bathroom went silent, at least in Boon's mental capacity it was. At the same time, Gia leaned forward to let the water out, Boon grabbed the radio and dropped it, still plugged in, into the tub with Gia. The Weekend had just finished the line, "…so, girl, what you singing fo'…" when the radio hit the water and the blue current, instantly, began to fry Gia, as if she was hickory-smoked bacon. Boon stepped back and watched, as Gia's body jumped and sizzled as it burned from the inside out. Her eyes burst and foam oozed from her mouth. The entire house lost power for a split second, and then it came back on. When Boon finally got his mind back, the tub was full of blood. He began to wipe down any surface his hands touched and he prepared to leave Gia's house. He was now ready for Zo.

At 1:17 a.m., Boon walked out of Gia's house, dialing the activation code for his prepaid phone. He was walking away from a gruesome murder he had not long ago committed, and was calmly trying to get back home, as if he'd had too much to drink at a neighborhood bar.

"Yellow Cab Company, may I help you?" asked the dispatcher.

Boon gave the woman his coordinates, as he stopped in front of a gas station, deciding to walk in. The dispatcher informed Boon that his cab would be there shortly, after he gave the dispatcher his prepaid cell number, before hanging up. While he was in the store, he approached the counter to purchase some Tylenol for his now throbbing head.

"Can I get a pack of Tylenol, two Dutch Masters cigarillos, and a box of Milk Duds?" Boon asked, reaching for the candy rack beneath the counter. Carefully, Boon made sure he grabbed cash from his wallet, instead of his card.

When Gia was found dead in her home, he
didn't want his cards to put him close to the area
around that time.

Minutes later, Boon's ringing prepaid
cellphone alerted him to his cab's impending
arrival. They were the only ones who had the
number. He walked out the store and hopped in
the cab.

"Where to, my man?" the fat, Italian driver
asked.

Boon slid the driver a hundred-dollar bill and
said, "Cabrini Green." The driver had a puzzled
look on his face, and understandably so. Cabrini
Green housing project was abandoned, after all.
"Don't worry, I am getting picked up by a friend
who lives nearby. They just didn't want to travel
this far from home and leave their kids
unattended," Boon lied. The driver nodded, then
shrugged, and began the trip.

Boon's head was throbbing, even more now,
and he realized he hadn't bought anything to
wash down the Tylenol. There was no way he
could take them without any liquid, so he'd have
to endure the pain for now.

"Hello?" the cabbie answered his phone via
the Bluetooth that was in his ear. "I'm workin'.
What the fuck do you think I'm doin'?" the
driver spat to his caller. "You don't believe me?

I believed you when you said you were only friends with that Bobby character, and look how that turned out!" he continued.

Boon wasn't paying him any attention, but he couldn't help but to think that all women were triflin'. Maybe he should've been one of those doggish, *only want one thing* kind of guys. He grimaced, as he pulled out his personal phone, searching through Facebook again.

"That broad's a tool too, and you wanna take advice from her?" the driver laughed, sarcastically. "Well, see me in fucking court then, Pamela. Until then, you and Christine, you's both can blow me. Goodbye, toots!" The driver hung up his call. "Un-fuckin-believable!" he huffed, loudly, as they neared Boon's destination. "Excuse me, sir?" The driver was looking at Boon in the rearview mirror now. "You seem like you're quite the ladies' man, but you ever have problems with two women at once?" the man asked. Boon laughed, hysterically. He tried to hold it in, but failed miserably.

The driver was uncertain how to feel towards his unyielding laughter. He just drove on, hoping and waiting for a reply.

When Boon calmed himself enough to speak, he said, "What's ya name, buddy?"

The driver looked in the rearview mirror to see if he was serious or about to crack a joke. "My name is Vincenzo. Vincenzo Betulli," the driver said.

Boon put his phone away. "Well, Vince; can I call you Vince?" Boon asked. Vincenzo nodded. "Women are 99.9% emotional, and when men don't cater to them 100%, women cause problems. Me, I'm saying, fuck 'em all!" Boon chuckled, as he thought about Lil, Mela, and now Gia.

"You go gay now?" Vince inquired.

"Fuck no!" Boon shot back. "Just what I said, fuck 'em. Stop caring and being all lovey-dovey, Vince; just *fuck* them," Boon emphasized. "When your feelings get involved, it makes room for you to have problems." Boon spoke from experience.

Vince nodded, as if he was taking it all in. "Okay," he began. "...but what would you do if you were in a relationship with one, and not only does she cheat on you, but her cheating gets her pregnant as well?" Vincenzo stopped the cab in front of the old housing project. Boon's headache was gone now. Boon was seething all over again. An infidelity that produced pregnancy had destroyed what he and Zo had. He loved her, but like all the other women he

250

loved, her pussy wasn't only for him. Boon remembered his siblings laughing at him. CiCi even had something to say about it. Had it not been for the darkness in the car, Vincenzo would have been able to see how red Boon had turned. The thought of the DNA results of baby Daniel was assaulting his mental faculties. He wanted to find Zo even more now.

"Sir!" the driver yelled, snapping Boon out of his trance. "I didn't mean to startle you, but we are here, sir," Vince said, noticing that Boon jumped when he'd yelled out to him.

Boon was so engulfed in his anger that he had pulled out another hundred-dollar bill and attempted to pay Vincenzo again.

"You paid already, sir," Vincenzo said, waving his hand in dismissal. Boon slid the bill back into his pocket and pulled the door handle to exit the vehicle. "Sir, you did not answer my question." The driver caught Boon before he could close the door. "What would you do about the cheating woman who got pregnant when she cheated?" Vince asked, again.

Boon's face twitched, as he leaned inside the car, looking over the seat at the cabbie. When Boon locked eyes with him, his face already said what was about to come out of his mouth. "Kill her," Boon said, with great conviction, and closed the door of the cab.

Boon called another cab company and had them meet him four blocks from where Vincenzo dropped him off. This cabbie drove him back to Lake Michigan to his Tahoe, and then he drove back to his parents' house. As he headed back north, his primary cellphone began to ring. When he looked at the screen and saw Deysha's face, he was tempted to let it go to voicemail, but he answered it. "Yeah?"

"What's up, baby brother?" Deysha asked, as if she was a saint.

Boon's eyebrows furrowed. "Shit," he said dryly, with a dollar shot of attitude.

"Aww, come on, I know you still ain't tripping off that old shit," Deysha said.

"What you on my line for, Deysha?" Boon asked, ready to end the call on her.

"I'm bored. Let's head out before you go back to Houston," Deysha said.

Boon scowled a bit and then smirked. "Not for lack of wanting to cuss you out!" Boon hung up. "These fucking women. God, please don't give me any daughters. She gonna make some man mad as a motherfucker one day, and I'ma have to kill him," he muttered to himself, as he drove on.

Three days had passed and Boon had just found out hours ago that Zo was back in Connecticut with her mom. After visualizing the tussle with Zo at the hotel, her participation in crushing the wedding reception, and the papers proving he hadn't fathered little Daniel, Boon had convinced himself to make the 13-hour drive to Hartford.

"Fuck it, the bitch gotta leave here," he told his reflection in the rearview mirror, as he backed out of his parents' driveway.

Just as he got to the end of the driveway, CiCi's Audi TT pulled alongside the curb. Boon saw her and she began to approach the passenger side window, trying to talk. He pulled off, leaving her screaming, inaudibly, behind him. His music was too loud for him to hear her.

"You gon' get yours too. Just you wait," he said, watching her fade in his rearview. He wasn't sure, but it appeared she was pointing at her car; however, Boon wasn't trying to stop for shit she had going on.

Boon made it to Hartford around 10 a.m. Although it was early spring, it was cold as shit. Boon's main objective was to see Zo take her last breath. She had humiliated him and he was beyond any type of reconciliation. He thought about little Daniel and the thought was bittersweet. Boon loved kids and would've been proud to be the little guy's father, but she'd denied him the pleasure. He Googled information on great views and scenery in Connecticut. He was hoping to be alone with Zo, and prior to doing so, he wanted to find a great spot. He also found a place to rent a car. He definitely didn't want his truck to be seen at all. He parked his truck in a paid parking garage and paid for three days. He didn't plan to be there for three days, but was being cautious.

Boon picked up the rental car and headed towards the South Hartford, middle-class neighborhood Zo lived in. As Boon approached the house, he noticed a young kid shooting basketball on a rim affixed over the garage. The boy was light-skinned, from what Boon could see, and well-covered in the cold, East Coast air. Boon pulled into the driveway of what appeared to be an empty house. He watched, as the boy shot a jump shot and it missed. He thought of how he hadn't gone through his childhood able to enjoy things by himself. Boon loved Dooly and Drakus, but they used to bully him. Recently, Deysha had begun to dig into Boon's bad side.

The young boy must have been called to go inside, because he dropped his ball and ran in the front door. Boon backed out of the driveway and eased closer to Zo's house. Thus far, he had avoided anyone spotting him at any of the murder scenes, and he was hoping to keep up with that trend. The front door opened again and Boon noticed a bundled-up Zo emerge. Boon was glad to see she had left the young man in the house. He pulled even closer now and let the passenger window down, as Zo walked down the sidewalk.

"Hey, beautiful. Can we talk?" Boon said, with a smile spreading across his face.

"I don't talk to strangers," Zo said. She glanced in Boon's direction, but didn't look long enough to look in his face.

"Oh, so now I'm a stranger?" Boon said.

Zo stopped. Boon was staring at Zo's ass. She was a walking contradiction to the fallacy of white girls not having big asses. Zo peered into the window for a few moments, this time. "I know that's not who I think it is!" Zo exclaimed, not believing her eyes.

Boon smiled a crocodile smile. "Who you think it is?"

"Boon, what you doing here? I thought you was married," Zo's tone was accusatory, as she stood there with her hands on her hips.

"I missed you," Boon lied. "I was hoping we could hang out and I could make up for being a jerk," he said.

Zo was taken aback, at first. "Are you serious? You know how shit went during our last get-together." Zo's body language showed that she wanted to go, even as she asked.

"Don't tell me I drove 13 hours, directly to your mom's address, to see ya fine-ass walking outside and now you done got scared?" Boon pressured her.

Zo came to the vehicle and climbed in. "You know I ain't never been a spooky broad," she said, as she buckled up. Boon turned the car around and drove them away.

"So where we going?" Zo asked Boon, as he handed her a cigarillo and a small bag of weed to roll up.

"I was hoping we could have a mini picnic. Let's find us a place to camp, in the car of course, and patch things up," Boon was lying on the fly now. He hadn't thought of a plan yet, but he was in mid-stride.

Zo put the finishing touches on the blunt. "Sounds good to me, baby. I just feel bad we hadn't done this long ago," Zo said.

"We need to stop by a store and grab some things, and then we can do it. I heard of some serene mountain views we could have our picnic at," Boon said.

Zo laughed, as she hit the blunt. "Boy, ya ass from Chicago. What you know about mountains?" she asked, sarcastically.

Boon laughed. "Nothing really. But at least we can have a first time event with each other," Boon commented.

Zo smiled at that and sat back. She was happy to be in Boon's company right now. She didn't ask about his wife. In fact, she could care less where his wife was or how she felt.

Before reaching a seemingly, uncharted, mountainous terrain, Boon had stopped by a grocery store and a package store. At the grocery store, he had given Zo $25 and told her to grab some food items for their picnic, while he remained in the car. When they went to the package store, Boon gave Zo another $50 and told her to grab them something to drink, her choice of liquor. Again, Boon remained in the car. Zo asked why he didn't come in and Boon simply said, "I gotta call a couple of clients before we get all wrapped up in our li'l rendezvous." In actuality, he didn't want to be caught on camera with her in any of the locations they stopped at.

After driving for what seemed an eternity, Boon found an isolated, wooded area that overlooked a pristine stream.

"You picked a crazy-ass place to picnic," Zo said, noting the lack of civilization.

"Let's just say I felt spontaneous and wanna see ya tattoo again," Boon winked. He was talking about the tattoo of his name emblazoned on her bottom.

She blushed. "So we fuckin' in the car, right?" Zo asked, as Boon put the car in park and put the seat back.

"Of course. It's too cold up here to have them ass cheeks out." They both had to laugh.

"I have a question," Zo stated, opening a bag of Ruffles Cheddar & Sour Cream chips. "So what happens after this? After we talk? After I put this pussy on you?" Zo rubbed her hand across his crotch.

Boon felt awkward. His penis reacted, as it should, but his mind was set on bitch-slapping Zo. "I want to make whatever Zora Tucker wants to happen, happen." Boon was still contemplating on how he would end her cunning existence. He applied a crooked smile and grabbed a few chips.

"What if I want what you gave Amy?" Zo asked, as she unwrapped and bit into a sub she bought from the deli of the grocery store.

Boon looked puzzled. "You mean, Amerie?" he quizzed. He'd never even remotely told Zo her name before.

"Yeah. Deysha said to just call her Amy," Zo said. She didn't' know that Boon hadn't had a decent conversation with his sister in over a year.

She turned to Zo, as he opened the cooler in the backseat, got a few ice cubes, and put them in both of their plastic cups. He opened the Amaretto Cîroc. "I bet my sister's 'ol jealous-ass made y'all crash the reception too, huh?" Boon asked, halfway filling the two cups with the vodka. He then opened one of the Cherry Cokes and began to pour it into the ice and liquor.

Zo sipped her drink, after stirring it with her finger first. "You know she did. I didn't even know you was getting married, let alone where you lived," Zo said solemnly, and then took another sip of her drink.

Boon was wondering what in the hell had gotten into Deysha. She was his favorite sibling. Now, it was as if she wanted to see Boon hurt, alone, and suffering. *But why?*

"If you ask me, it seems like she got some kind of trick up her sleeve. How the hell...Naw, why bring all your exes to crash yo' shit?" Zo asked, sipping on the liquid courage again.

Boon couldn't answer that question, and he had a look of hot red on his face.

Zo noticed and tried to lighten the mood. "So, Mr. Spontaneous, what's up with me, you, and this picnic?" Zo finished her cup. She was a drinker, so this early indulging was a small thing to a giant.

"Hang on a sec. You mind getting a little air wit' a nigga?" Boon asked, as he got out of the car. He was concealing a hunting knife, under his waistband, which he'd taken from his father's collection before leaving Chicago.

"Boy, it's colder than a penguin's dick out there. Ain't no li'l air. It's a whole lotta—" Boon's abrupt closing of the car door cut off Zo's comment.

Boon stood on the rugged outback in the crisp breeze, still thoughtless as to what Deysha's intentions were. A plethora of things played in his mind; especially, the inevitable murders of his remaining exes, including Zo.

"Damn, it's fuckin' freezing. I hope li'l Daniel stayed in the house like I told him," Zo said, as she stopped and stood beside Boon.

The statement was in Boon's ears like nails on a chalkboard. It made him feel the evil, the hate, the malice he had begun to feel before leaving Houston.

"You okay?" Zo asked, when she saw Boon's facial expression. He looked as though he was seeing an arch nemesis of his.

Boon blew out a long wind of frustration. "Come here, ma," Boon said, as he pulled her in front of him. He turned her back to him and pulled her closer. Her soft, plump ass was against his wood and the vanilla cream scent from her shampoo filled his nostrils. Zo wasn't inebriated, but she was definitely feeling her earlier drink.

"Women think men can't feel pain, or at least should just *man up* and press on. But when a woman gets her feelings hurt or her heart broken, then it's hell to tell the captain," Boon said, with tears filling his eyes. He put his left arm around Zo's chest and embraced her. "The fucked up part is, you are all God's gift to us, so why hurt the good guys?" he asked her, rhetorically.

Zo, although Boon couldn't see it, had become teary-eyed as well. "Boon, I was young. I knew what I had in you, but I allowed myself to believe that I was lonely," Zo said, and Boon could feel her tears plop on his left hand.

He moved her hair from her neck and kissed her there. Still embracing her with his left hand, he used the right to pull out the hunting knife. "That was a defining moment in my life, Zo. That shit scarred my brain's ability to trust," Boon said. He felt more of Zo's tears hit his hand. "You ever been stabbed in the back, Zo?" Boon asked, now violently tightening the once-passionate embrace.

"Boon, you're hurting me." Zo tried to wriggle free, but was no match for Boon's manly biceps.

"I wasn't able to tell you that shit when you was busting it open while I was away at school. Were you?" Boon spat, bringing his arm up to restrain Zo in a chokehold. "Now, you still haven't answered my question, Zo." Boon showed her the stainless steel blade.

Zo panicked, immediately. "Oh my God! Boon, please, baby! No, we have a son, Boon!" Zo pleaded. However, she said the words that lit the dynamite.

Boon lost it. "We? Bitch, we ain't got a muthafuckin' thing but a problem! This is what it feels like to be backstabbed, Zo!" Boon shot, as he swung the knife backwards. Zo struggled to scream, but Boon had a vice grip on her throat. She mouthed, *nooo*, as she felt the excruciating pain of the serrated steel penetrating her kidney.

"Before you die, ho, tell me how it feels! Bitches like backstabbing ol' Boon. How does being stabbed back feel? Huh?" Boon yelled, as he viciously stabbed Zo four more times. Her body went limp in his grip, while he was still wrapped in his silent state of malicious murder. Boon let her drop to the ground.

He went to the car for the bottle of Cîroc, which he proceeded to douse Zo's body with before lighting her on fire. As the fire gained life and ate its way up Zo's corpse, Boon found himself becoming more at ease. It was like a weight had just been lifted off of him. When he was done with Zo, he stripped off his bloody clothes, bagged them and tossed them into the trunk of the rental car. For a while he just sat in the rental with the heater running, reflecting on what he'd just done. A sinister smile spread across his face and he pulled away from the crime scene.

Boon's first destination was his truck, which he'd left in the parking garage about 15 miles from Zo's house. On the way, he saw a self-serve car wash and made a mental note to return after he'd changed. When he made it to his Tahoe, he dropped the soiled clothes inside and put on the socks, jeans, Timbs, and leather bomber he'd had inside. He was thankful that he had brought winter gear, or else he would've looked insane, wearing summer clothes as cold as it was. Boon drove the car to the car wash, cleaning it thoroughly.

Since he had to rent the car for a minimum of 24 hours, Boon chose to buy a parking pass for the day in the same garage he'd parked his SUV. He was assigned a space on the third floor. His truck was on the ground floor, which was perfect for him, just in case someone was nosy enough to notice him in the rental, as well as the Tahoe. He slept inside the midsize sedan, popping up at odd hours to crank the car and run the heater. Once it was time for him to get back to the Windy City, he washed the vehicle once again for good measure, even vacuuming the inside, and returned it without so much as a minor hiccup. He returned to his truck and drove off, headed back to his hometown. Taz was on his shit sheet next.

*

264

After a 13-hour, return drive, Boon entered Chicago. He was physically tired, and severely annoyed. He kept getting calls from both Amerie and CiCi. It pissed him off highly to think that the two of them were harassing him as if they hadn't done anything to him.

"So you still ain't trying to speak to me, nigga?" CiCi spat, sarcastically, sounding as if she wanted to cry.

"What the fuck we gotta talk about, Curelle? You lucky it ain't your turn yet!" Boon was beyond irritated and it slipped. Boon couldn't see CiCi through his phone, but if he could have, he would have seen an intrigued look on her face.

"What the hell is that supposed to mean? My turn for what?" CiCi's interest piqued.

Boon didn't answer right away. He loved her still, and killing her weighed heavily on his mind as well. But at the same time, he wasn't prepared to do that to his first love. "I'm going back to Houston after I handle this last li'l thang. Just stay away."

CiCi didn't let him finish. "Stop fuckin' runnin' from me, Boon," she said, causing him to remain on the phone. "You know like hell I never intended to hurt you. We were besties. The very best of everything, and now 'cause you mad at who-the-hell-ever, I get kicked too. Hell no. I won't take this one," Curelle spat, as she began to cry.

Boon felt the newly-formed icicles slowly falling off his heart. "CiCi, they hurt me. All of them. Even this bitch, Amerie." Boon thought, again, about the video of his wife and J.G. and he bit his lip so hard, he tasted blood. A warm tear made a path down his right cheek.

"What did the bitch do? You know I already wanna mud dog drag that ho." CiCi still thought about the gun Amerie pulled out on her. "I…they…Lil…Mela…" Boon fought back angry tears, and she tried to piece together what he was attempting to say, but nothing made sense. She had never heard Boon like this and it genuinely hurt her now. She was also hiding a huge secret, but it was clearly not the time for revelation. "Taz…man…that bitch almost got me killed! I never thought she would set me up. A nigga split my head open, because she let him in my house," Boon said. At this point, he was merely rambling on in anger. He hadn't given a second thought to the fact that he and CiCi were still on the phone.

"What!" CiCi yelled. "I knew something was up. It was the night you went to the hospital and tried to call me, huh?" CiCi's inquiry fell on deaf ears. Boon was a maniacal mess now.

"Oh yeah! Bitch gotta go," Boon's voice was flat. Before CiCi could ask anything else, Boon had already hung up. She didn't call back. She had something she needed to take care of. Her something to say could wait a bit longer.

Boon was livid and opted not to get any sleep. It had been eight days since he left Houston and he still had to carry out two more murders: Taz and CiCi's. He would kill Amerie when he got home. Boon was out of ideas and didn't bother with contemplating any. He used his cellphone to call Taz's last known number.

"Hello?" a man answered.

"I need to speak to Taz. Tatiyana Lopes," Boon requested.

"She called me a few months back and told me to give her new number to anyone that called looking for her. This no longer her line," the man said. He gave Boon the new number.

Boon hung up and promptly dialed. He was in his truck in Downtown Chicago. His mind was obsessed with doing treacherous things. He listened, impatiently, to the ringing phone in his ear. Voicemail. Boon didn't want to leave a message. He dialed again. "Bitch, I know yo' talking-ass gonna answer the fuckin' phone," he spat, as her line rang in his ear for the second time.

"Who is this?" Taz answered, with an attitude.

Boon smiled deviously. "I'm hopin' it's the nigga who can change the mood you in, Taz."

"Well, I'ma need a name first, nigga who hopes he can change my mood," Taz remarked.

"Still a firecracker I see." Boon wanted to choke this bitch through the phone, but he had to get his Denzel on so that she would roll with it.

Taz was baffled. There was only one man she knew who used the word firecracker to describe her. "Boon?" she guessed, with a smile in her voice.

"However did you know?" Boon asked, with a hint of sarcasm. Taz liked the surprise call, but thought about the last three times she saw Boon, and how very unpleasant those meetings had been. She'd gotten him robbed and assaulted, came to his office to lie about her involvement and give a counterfeit apology, and was a member of the *bitch party* that crashed his reception. Mostly, she remembered the pimp slap she received from Boon, like a sawed-off shotgun blast to the left side of her face. "You the only nigga who calls a bitch a firecracker. Besides, it's only one nigga wit' a voice so damn *playa* and a pimp hand so strong." Taz said. She sounded like she took enjoyment from it.

Boon thought, *if she liked that, then what I want to do to her would have her deathly infatuated.* "So look, I'm in Chicago. I wanna fuck wit' ya; whatcha say we let bygones be bygones and kick it a bit," Boon offered.

"Hmm… " Taz thought about it. She currently had a boyfriend, but Boon had turned into a beast, and something about it made her want him. "I'm housesitting for my friend. You can come through, but it's a guy, so let's not rumble in here." Taz had to chuckle at her statement. Boon was glad this was happening, but he knew Taz was a con artist. He knew to take the .357 with him and keep it handy.

"Gimme the address."

Boon pulled up to the address that Taz had given him on Marquette. He parked on the side of the curb, instead of the driveway, as she had instructed. Boon shut off the engine and put the revolver in his waistband. He was reaching for the door latch, when his phone rang. Boon hit ignore. He didn't want to hear any excuses. He didn't give a damn if her friend was on his way home. His ass would have to die too.

269

Boon walked up the driveway and to the front door. The house was a late-model, two-story, brick house in a mid to upper-class area. Boon grabbed the oversized knocker and tapped the door four times. Taz came to the door and pulled it open. "I was calling you to tell you just come in, crazy boy," she said, as she walked back to a chair where she'd been polishing her toenails. She was dressed in next to nothing, wearing a cut-off T-shirt and a pair of yellow Tommy Hilfiger shorts that were unbuttoned. Boon could tell that she had recently done her hair. It shimmered and looked good in an updo. The room smelled like oil sheen, and Boon noticed the can of oil sheen on the table by her nail polish.

"I'm done wit' my toes; just need 'em to dry, and then I'm all yours," Taz said, seductively. Boon had to admit to himself that she was truly a bad bitch. His plan was to kill her, but he would give her the dick for the road.

Boon and Taz smoked several blunts, as she talked about no longer being money hungry. She told him she had settled down and that he had power-slapped her into being a decent woman. Taz opened a bottle of Ace of Spades, and they sipped and tripped. Boon constantly looked around and watched the lock on the front door.

Taz was a triflin' muthafucka and he didn't trust her.

"Turn on some music," Boon told her. Taz nodded and went to the radio. When she turned it on, Ginuwine's "Pony" was on and Taz came out of her Tommy shorts. This was the song playing when they had sex for the first time. Boon noticed that Taz didn't have on any type of panties. *This freak*, he thought. Taz, sexily, made her way towards Boon and he couldn't wait. She straddled Boon and began to rock and sway to the beat. Boon took that as an invitation. Her perky breasts were in his face, their nipples looking in his eyes. He raised her shirt and she helped him take it off. Boon bit her chin, playfully, and then alternated kissing and sucking each nipple. Taz moaned, as she felt Boon's dick stiffen through his Akoo jeans.

"I want that dick, Boon. Please," Taz begged. She stood up and unzipped his pants. Boon lifted his shirt, took out his .357, and sat it on the table. Taz only smiled and gave him a look that said she understood.

Taz, instantly, bent over and took Boon's thickness into her mouth. Boon loved the way she sucked dick. He was still going to kill her; but for now, he wanted to kill that mouth. "Mmm... That's right. Be bad, Taz," Boon said.

He leaned forward in the chair, as Taz worked her magic, and smacked her ass hard.

Taz moaned, "Mmm hmm…" Taz stood up and Boon slid on a Magnum. Taz sat on the stiff rod and it nearly took her breath away. "Oh. I miss it. I do, Boon," Taz moaned, as she bounced in Boon's lap. Taz's new boyfriend was incomparable to Boon, and she needed this in her life. "Ooo, ooh, fuck me! Damn!" Taz rolled her hips and rocked on Boon's length. Her body quivered from her mounting orgasm. "Choke me, Daddy," she screamed, and Boon gladly obliged. He grabbed her by her throat and her ass, then stood up, still stroking, and pinned her to the wall.

"That's…what…I'm…talking…'bout…lem me…beat…that…" Boon emphasized each word with a long, hard stroke. He pounded Taz's walls, as she came back-to-back.

"Oh, yesssss, Boon. I'm cummin' so fuckin hard!" Taz seemed to have a seizure on Boon's dick, as he let his man juice go as well. His ass muscles were tight from the stroking, but he was well satisfied.

He walked Taz to a chair and sat her in it. "Now, for some fun," Boon said. "I know you got some stockings. You never go without them," Boon said. It was true; she wore lots of dresses, and always had stockings to go with them. She was interested in what Boon was planning on doing, but she knew he was a Scorpio and very sporadic with his spontaneity.

"They're in my bag by the couch." Boon grabbed her bag and took out a pair of black, sheer pantyhose. He went into the kitchen, and unbeknownst to Taz, cut the legs of them apart and then cut each leg in half. Taz, ready for another round, looked as Boon emerged from the kitchen. She didn't move, as he began to tie her hands and feet to the chair. She went along with it. In fact, she was getting even more aroused because of the restraints. "I have been a bad girl, you gon' punish me?" she seductively asked Boon.

"You have no fuckin' idea," Boon said, as he tied the last stocking around her left ankle and the leg of the chair.

"Now, Taz," Boon spoke, as he stood. "I have a confession to make. Remember when you lied about not being involved with the niggas who came and robbed me?" Boon asked.

Taz, immediately, panicked and felt her heart rate climb at a dangerous pace. "Daniel, I'm sorry."

Boon looked at Taz with venom in his eyes. "Shut the fuck up!" he spat. "All you hoes is sorry, when a nigga come to get his muthafuckin' straightenin'." Boon didn't want to shoot Taz. The gunshot would alert the neighbors. "Like I was saying before yo' *sorry-ass* interrupted me. Just like you lied to me, I lied to you. I said let bygones be bygones," Boon chuckled. He grabbed the oil sheen off the table. "Shiiiit. You gotta pay me for that," Boon said, digging in his pocket.

Taz was absolutely spooked. "B-B-Boon. Please…I…I didn't know." Taz was crying. She saw hell in Boon's eyes moments ago, and now again when he said, "You like doing hot shit, Taz. I mean, you a hot bitch!" Boon brandished the lighter. He could remember watching Zo burn and the gratifying feeling it sent through his body as she went up in flames. Boon flicked the lid up on the lighter. He got close to Taz's body and she blew it out. "Please, Boon! I'm begging you! Don't do this. I fucked up, okay? Is that what you want? I got money, baby. I won't tell the cops, or nothing; just please, let me go." Taz knew shit had gotten real. Boon flicked the flame up again, and again, Taz blew it out.

Boon slapped fire from Taz's face. "Blow my shit out again and I'm stabbing you in the asshole wit' a butcher knife!" Boon spat.

274

Flicking up the flame for a third time, intending to ignite Taz's hair. He reached out, only to have her blow it out again. Exasperated, Boon grabbed the can of oil sheen. This time when he lit the flame, he sprayed the oil sheen over the lighter and the fireball hit Taz right in the face. She howled, as the inferno caught in her hair and melted her skin. Boon let the flame down. "I like doin' hot shit too, you bitch," Boon spat. "You know what they say," he continued, as Taz floated in and out of consciousness. Her body badly burned and still smoking, Boon hit her with the oil sheen fireball again. "You play with fire, it'll fuck yo' dumbass up. Burn in hell wit' ya hot-ass." Boon put fire to the curtains in the living room and then untied Taz. He grabbed his clothes, dressed and put his gun on his waist. He opened the door with his T-shirt. He took one last look at what used to be one beautiful woman. She'd brought this on herself, he reasoned. She had shown her ugly side to the wrong nigga. His heart was broken, and so was his sense of reasoning.

Kill Switch

Boon sped away from the home, after setting the living room on fire. He was ready to talk to CiCi, but he had cruel intentions. As he neared Madison, he pulled out his phone to make the call. His hands shook, as he scrolled through his call log for her phone number. Boon waited, as CiCi's call tone sang in his ear, only to roll to voicemail. Boon tried her eight, consecutive times, but still, no answer. Boon was seething now. As much as she had been blowing his line up for the past year, now she wouldn't answer. "Bitch probably out givin' up the pussy too," Boon said aloud, as he headed towards CiCi's last known address.

CiCi sat in IHOP, eating their famous Rooty Tooty Fresh 'N Fruity breakfast and using her laptop connected to the restaurant's Wi-Fi. While she was searching online, she and Deysha had been arguing for the last 20 minutes about why the hell Deysha was intent on hurting Boon.

"Look, ho, I been here forever. You just a bitch he had fucked wit'," Deysha said.

"You sound just as bad as one of his crazy-ass exes. That's probably why ya ol' man got the fuck on. Dizzy-ass broad!" CiCi snarled into the phone. She was pissed that she'd let Deysha talk her into crashing that reception and that she'd let Deysha invite Amerie to Boon's house during their chill and smoke session.

"I got one fa you. Don't let us run into each other no time soon, bitch!" Deysha spat, venomously, before hanging up. CiCi was in a daze. *This ho betta act like she know, or Boon gon' be a sibling short*, she thought.

CiCi was scrolling down the webpage she was looking at and finally found what she was looking for. "Yeah, ho, it's game time." CiCi wiped her mouth, took a sip of water, grabbed her check, and paid for her food. Before leaving the restaurant, she made sure she programmed the number she'd searched for in her phone. CiCi got in her Audi Coupe and turned over the ignition. As her engine purred, she took a deep breath. She let down her drivers' window to let in some of the warm, spring air. The sun was glaring off her phone screen, so she put on her Dolce & Gabbana shades. She had six more missed calls from Boon, this morning alone. He had called her nine times last night, but she had to book her flight. CiCi dialed the number she programmed in her phone under *POW*.

"Attorney Amerie D. Watson, may I help you?" Amerie greeted.

CiCi hated the sound of this bitch's voice. She wanted to go ballistic, but kept her emotions in check and said, "Good morning, Mrs. Watson. My name is Kaycee Andrews and I have a very high-profile case about to take place. You came highly recommended and I won't settle for less than your services." CiCi's face screwed up in a disgusted scowl.

"Ma'am, while I thank you for your compliments, I am taking a personal leave of absence, so that I can deal with a few issues of my own," Amerie replied. "I can, however, refer you to—"

CiCi interrupted her. "I only want to deal with you, Mrs. Watson. I know there are some great attorneys. I have $15,000 up front, cash, and will fully cover whatever other expenses I will incur through your services."

Amerie contemplated the offer. Fifteen thousand sounded good right now. Besides, if Boon was going to leave her for good, she needed to run up a good piece of change to stash. "Where are you located?" Amerie asked.

CiCi inhaled, sharply, and smiled. "I'm in Indiana now, but I'll be in Houston by 5 p.m. today."

Amerie took a deep breath of her own this time. "If you can get to my office by 6 p.m. today, we can meet then. If not— "

CiCi interjected, "I'll be there."

"Sounds great. See you this evening, Ms. Andrews," Amerie said, and then hung up the phone.

CiCi's smile grew wider than the Grinch, and she pulled away from the IHOP.

As soon as CiCi got home, she rushed to get her clothes together and headed to the airport for her four-hour flight. As she sat in the terminal waiting to board her flight, her phone rang; it was Boon, again. "Yes, sir?" she said, finally answering.

"Yo, where you at?" Boon asked, in a most intolerant tone.

"Sorry, Boon. You already waived the right to ask me questions like that. What you need though?" she asked, playfully.

Boon clenched his teeth together. "I wanted to talk to you before I got back to Houston," he said, trying not to sound as pissed off as he was.

CiCi used this as her opportunity to get some information from him. "I mean, what time you goin' back to H-Town?" she asked.

Boon was actually at the entrance ramp to the expressway, so he pulled over and said, "I was leaving now, but I can wait until I see you first," he said.

"I thought it would be a few days or so from now. I guess I can call you when I'm done with my li'l problem." CiCi was mocking him, jokingly, but he didn't catch on.

"Whatever, Curelle." Boon hung up and began his 16-hour road trip back to the Lone Star State.

CiCi was in the air, on her way to Texas. She was able to flirt with the airport security guard and get on the plane with a .45 she obtained and registered in her name after her last run-in with Amerie. The security guard hand-frisked CiCi, spending much of his attention on her ample breasts and ass, but neglecting to check her purse or use the wand on her. As she sat back to think about what she was about to do, she dozed off into a temporary slumber.

"Welcome to George Bush Intercontinental Airport, ma'am," the flight attendant's voice awakened CiCi, after they'd landed in Texas. CiCi had booked a rental car for her stay and headed for the kiosk, immediately after stepping off the plane.

CiCi was in her rental car, heading towards Amerie and Boon's Harris County law firm. Upon arrival, CiCi noticed there was only one car outside, which gave her a little more comfort. It was close to 6, so before getting out of the vehicle, CiCi called Amerie again. After verifying that Amerie was still inside, and the BMW 745 outside belonged to her, CiCi chambered a round in her .45 and exited her rented Toyota Avalon. As she approached the building, she saw a sign beside the door with a picture of Boon and Amerie, smiling in an advertisement of their family practice. CiCi reached into her purse, slid on a pair of latex gloves, and opened the door to step in the office. Amerie sat with her head down, looking at something she was writing on her desk. Without looking up, she said, "I'll be with you in just a second, Ms. Andrews."

CiCi chuckled to herself a bit and replied, "We got time". Amerie had on a tan skirt and a white blouse, her hair was pulled back in a ponytail. She was pretty and confident of it. CiCi was anxious to beat her ass, but she waited. CiCi, wearing a pair of Polo shorts, a Mickey Mouse T-shirt and a pair of white, low-top Air Force Ones, was dressed to kick some ass. "How may I help you?" Amerie said, before lifting her head.

"Lemme get one before I take your life," CiCi said, making eye contact with Amerie.

Amerie didn't seem the least bit shocked. "I don't know how I knew, but I did. Something told me you were gonna be back, sooner than later, to try this shit." Amerie smirked.

CiCi was getting angrier with every passing second. "Oh, you think it's a game? All you ratchet hoes tried my boy like a lame, but you the only bitch that had the audacity to try me. I'm finna get in yo' ass about pullin' that pistol on me!" CiCi yelled.

"Oh, really? I know your type, CiCi. Been dealin' wit scallywags like you since high school. I'm prettier, got more money, more sexual, and my pussy is the bomb." Amerie stood up. "While I enjoy seeing you hoes cry over me taking my husband, I got better shit to do with my time, right now," she said.

CiCi hawk spit in Amerie's face. "That's how I feel about you and ya hot-ass pussy, you gotdamn cum-dumpster! One of us ain't leavin' here. Believe that!" CiCi yelled.

Amerie now noticed that CiCi was wearing gloves. Amerie began taking off her earrings. CiCi was taller and bigger than she was, but she was no bear and Amerie was not a scary bitch.

"Okay, now that's what I'm talking about," CiCi said, getting ready to sit her purse down. CiCi saw Amerie sit her earrings on the desk, but she quickly snatched open her desk drawer. "I knew yo' sneaky-ass was gonna try that bullshit." CiCi stepped up and pressed her .45 against Amerie's cheek. "Close the drawer, slowly." CiCi told her.

"I thought we were supposed to be fightin'. What's with the gun?" Amerie asked, as she pushed the drawer closed.

"You changed the rules when you tried to get ya li'l peashooter out ya desk." CiCi moved the gun from Amerie's cheek, but when Amerie turned to face her, she struck Amerie in the face with the butt of the pistol. The blow hit Amerie in the mouth and broke her two, front teeth.

Amerie's mouth dripped blood, as she screamed, "You fuckin' fat bitch! Look what you did to my— " CiCi slapped Amerie with the gun again, this time, across the bridge of her nose. Amerie fell back into her desk, grabbing her nose and howling in pain.

"Shut that shit up, ho. Ain't hear none of that weak-ass cryin' when you had ya li'l double deuce aimed at me; you was poppin' shit then. I guess it ain't no fun when the rabbit got the gun, huh?" CiCi asked, rhetorically.

"You won't get away with this shit," Amerie mumbled, barely audible. Her nose and mouth were still bleeding profusely, and she struggled to breathe, let alone speak. "Did I ask you to say something, ho?" CiCi slapped Amerie in the forehead with the gun, this time. "That's what's wrong wit' you prissy bitches. Don't know when to be quiet!" she said. "Now, you got a choice. Either you a heartless broad or you fucked in the head. Wherever yo' issue at, we gon' end that today. So, head or heart?" CiCi asked.

Amerie began to sob. She had a knot on her forehead that looked as if her brain was laying an ostrich egg.

"Please, CiCi. I—" CiCi feigned a swing of the gun again, and Amerie threw her hands up, as if to block the blow. CiCi laughed at her feeble attempt to protect herself. "Heeeeelp!" Amerie screamed.

She opened her mouth to scream again and CiCi inserted the .45, hollering, "I told you, y'all hoes don't know when to quit. Don't know how to close ya legs or ya muthafuckin' mouth." CiCi was beyond annoyed.

Amerie began to plead again, with her eyes streaming tears.

BOOM!

CiCi pulled the trigger, and instantly, the back of Amerie's head was splattered against the painting on the wall. "Guess you gonna keep that mouth close fa'sho now," CiCi said to Amerie's dead body.

Taking several tissues from the box on Amerie's desk, she wiped the blood from her gun, before putting it back in her purse. She searched Amerie's purse until she found her driver's license. She smiled, as she read the address. She walked out of the office and got into her rental.

The GPS directions to Boon and Amerie's home were accurate, with the time it estimated CiCi would take getting there. As she pulled into the driveway, she saw a garage on both sides of the house and hoped no one was home. She walked to the front door and rang the doorbell. There was no answer, so she rang twice more and still got no answer. She walked around to the back of the house and tapped on a window by the back door. After convincing herself that the house was empty, she took out her gun and used the butt to smash the window. She reached inside, unlocked the window, and climbed inside.

The home instantly made her jealous. This is what she and Boon should've had; not the slut he had chosen to marry. On the way over to Boon's house, CiCi got rid of the latex gloves and bought two roses: one red and one black.

She went into the kitchen and got two, tall glasses from the cabinet. After filling them both half full with water, she put a rose in each, and sat them on the dining room table. She went into Boon's living room, sat on the couch, and turned on the television to play the waiting game.

*

CiCi had been in Boon's house for hours, without even a phone call. She had gone to sleep on his couch around 7 in the evening, and here it was, now the wee hours of the morning. She woke up to pee and remembered that she hadn't parked the Toyota on the curb. Boon would know someone was at his house. *Fuck it*, CiCi thought, as she used the restroom. After flushing the toilet and repositioning herself on the couch, she could hear the garage on the left side of the house open. She knew it was Boon, and her hands began to perspire. She pulled her .45 out of her purse, chambered a round, and sat it in her lap. She muted the TV, so she could hear when he drew near. The garage door closed, and so did the driver's door to a vehicle. Moments later, she heard the kitchen door that led from the garage, open and close. CiCi was anxious, but she made an attempt to steel her nerves.

"Amerie?" Boon called out his wife's name.

CiCi scowled.

Boon came into the living room where CiCi was. He had followed the light from the television.

"Hello, Daniel," CiCi greeted him from the couch.

Boon damn near jumped out of his drawers. "What the hell you doin' here? Where the fuck is Amerie?" Boon asked, trying to regain his composure.

"Me," CiCi began, "I'm here to get some straightenin'. As far as that skanch you married, I been told you I don't keep up wit' ya hoes." Boon's eyebrows furrowed. He began to walk towards CiCi. She raised her gun and pointed it at Boon. "Sit down," she instructed.

"What? You gon' shoot me now?" Boon asked, not sold on the fact that she would.

"I might," CiCi calmly said. Boon took another step towards her.

BLAM!

CiCi shot the floor in front of his feet. "Sit yo' ass down, Daniel. Damn!" CiCi spat. Reluctantly, Boon sat down. He was in a volatile state, but CiCi had a banger and he wasn't about to try her gangsta. "So, Daniel, this is what I gotta do to get you to sit still and talk to ya *best friend*?" CiCi asked.

"Man, this can't be what the fuck you really want, Curelle. And how the fuck you know where I rest at?" Boon spat.

"Okay. I'll get to the point. What's up wit' Lil and Mela?" CiCi asked. Boon made the most hateful face she'd ever seen on him. "Come on, Boon. This me," CiCi urged.

Boon shifted in his seat. "Them hoes got what they deserved." Boon said, matter-of-factly.

"Hmm. And Taz too, huh? And Gia?" CiCi probed.

Boon nodded.

"Were you comin' for me too, Daniel? Is that what 'you lucky you ain't next' was for?" she asked, recalling what Boon had said when he answered her call two days ago.

"Curelle, y'all fucked a nigga head up. All this playin' and hot in the ass shit." Boon let a teardrop slide, unchecked, down his cheek.

In a crazy way, CiCi could feel his pain. "Boon, I've always loved you. I just thought I was losing the best thing I ever had, to yet another tramp. Then, you gave me the best of anything a girl could ever ask for." CiCi dropped a tear now as well.

"Get outta here wit' all that. So the dick was good. You ain't gotta put all the extras on it," Boon said, waving her off.

CiCi shook her head. "Boon, I gave birth to a son - your son - on December 4th. His name is Dietrich Omir; and yes, he is yours, before you even attempt to ask. The last man I had been with, before you, was three months before me and you," CiCi admitted, solemnly.

Boon was at a loss for words. He felt in his heart of hearts that CiCi was telling him the truth. "I know you got pictures, Curelle. Lemme see him," Boon said, wiping his face.

She pulled her cellphone from her purse and went to the photos of young Dietrich. Boon took a deep breath and exhaled. CiCi handed him the phone, so he could see his son.

"He was in the car wit' me when you pulled off on me at ya mama's house that day, too," CiCi said.

Boon was captivated by the resemblance he saw to himself in the infant's pictures. CiCi joined him on the couch, and late night gave way to early morning, as the two chatted away.

Ding! Dong!

The doorbell startled both him and CiCi. They had dozed off on the couch, watching *I'm*

Gonna Git You Sucka. Boon hopped up and went to the door.

"Who is it?" he asked, as CiCi got up and went to use the restroom.

"Harris County Police."

Boon opened the door to two gents in slacks and button-ups, flashing gold badges. The tall, chubby guy spoke first.

"Good morning, sir. I am Detective Rollins and this is Detective Myers. Are you Daniel Watson?" the detective asked. Boon was uncertain of what was going on, but nodded. "I'm afraid we have some bad news, sir. Your wife, Amerie Watson, was found dead this morning in your office." The shorter detective, an expert on body language, watched, carefully, for Boon's reaction.

Boon was genuinely shocked and it showed.

"What the fuck! What happened?" he asked.

"Looks like a single gunshot wound to the face, from close range. Sir, I know this is a tough pill to swallow, but do you mind coming down to the station to answer a few questions for us?" the tall, chubby detective asked.

"Not at all. Let me grab my keys." Boon closed the door and went to find CiCi. "Aye, I need to go with—"

CiCi held her hand up to pause Boon, "I'll be right here when you get back. I heard them," she said.

"Don't go anywhere," Boon said.

He grabbed his keys off the table and went to the door. CiCi walked back to the living room. She looked at the two roses she had placed on the dining room table. She was hoping that they took on their meanings right now. The black rose was for death, not only for Amerie's death, but also for the death of CiCi being without Boon. The red rose was for love. Her love for Boon, for the future they possibly had, and for the life they'd created. At that moment, she thought of their son and smiled. She picked up her phone and its screen was still in her photo gallery of Dietrich's pictures. He was such a handsome little fellow.

CiCi was glad Boon had dealt with the other hoes. Now, it was only a matter of getting away with it. She felt confident she'd get away with spattering Amerie's brain matter all over her office wall.

"Fuck it. That bitch fucked with the wrong one."

CiCi turned on some cartoons and lay back down.

291

X'D OUT

Boon walked into the police station, on his own recognizance. Detective Rollins went to grab the trio some coffee and pastries, as Detective Myers led Boon into an interrogation room near the back of the precinct. Boon had been here on many different occasions prior, but always to come to the aid of a client being hassled by Harris County's finest.

Boon was seated in one of the plastic chairs and the slender, Detective Myers, sat in the chair across from him.

"Mr. Watson, can you think of anyone that would want to hurt your wife?" the clean-cut detective asked.

He had worked numerous cases similar to this one in his 14-year career. He'd seen all sorts of outcomes. Boon knew deep down that he, himself, wanted to murder Amerie, but had to admit that he couldn't think of anyone else.

"No. She didn't fuck with anybody," he said. The words "fuck with" lingered on his mind.

"Where were you yesterday between the hours of 4:30 p.m. and 8 o'clock p.m.?" Detective Myers asked, as Detective Rollins walked in with a dozen donuts and a cup holder with three cups of hot coffee. He sat the donuts on the table, slid Boon a cup of coffee, and took a seat at the table, next to his partner. Boon grabbed a half-and-half creamer and a few packets of sugar.

"I was in my truck, on the way here from Chicago. I've got gas and food purchase receipts to prove that as well," Boon said, as he dressed his coffee.

Detective Rollins decided to speak, as his partner fixed up a cup for himself. "Daniel, I'm about to show you a very disturbing image. I don't know if you know about it, but it may help the case," he said.

The detective pulled out Amerie's cellphone and played the video message she'd received from Lola. Boon instantly got pissed. He remembered the same message coming through to his phone.

"Yeah, I know about that," Boon said, with clenched teeth, and the detectives exchanged knowing looks.

"Mr. Watson, do you know the man in this video with your wife?" Detective Rollins asked.

Boon wanted to lie, but he unintentionally spoke the truth. "Yeah. He used to be my boy, until this video came to my phone almost two weeks ago."

"So, what is his name?" Myers asked, taking out his pen.

Boon wiped his hand down his face, as if he were wiping away his frustration. "Julius…Julius Glover. He works at the jail as a detention officer," Boon said honestly.

The detectives knew he was being truthful, because they had received confirmation that Amerie got the video message from a number belonging to London Glover.

"Okay, Mr. Watson, you're free to go." Detective Rollins slid him a card with his name and number on it. "Call me if anything else comes to mind. My partner will drive you home, if you're not okay to drive yourself," he said.

Boon took the card and stood from his seat. He was wondering who killed Amerie. Who took his satisfaction? Lola was mad at J.G.'s infidelity, but to kill like this?

"Detective Rollins," Boon looked at the seasoned veteran. "You have any photos of Amerie?" Boon asked.

"Right here." The detective, cautiously, spread several pictures across the table.

Amerie's once-beautiful face was mangled beyond recognition, and her body sprawled awkwardly across her desk chair. Boon liked the handiwork, but suppressed his pleasure.

"What… what the hell did that?" Boon asked. His facial expression twisted and he grimaced, as he looked away from the pictures.

"It was...a .45 caliber pistol," Myers said. Boon pretended to get sick. "Come on, Mr. Watson, I'll take you home." Myers guided Boon out of the interrogation room. "Give me your keys, we'll have an officer follow us in your vehicle to your house."

"I'm sorry for your loss, Daniel," Rollins called from behind them, as they left the station.

*

When Boon was dropped off in his driveway, he noticed that CiCi hadn't left. He was gratified, because he wanted to talk about his son some more. He walked inside and noticed that CiCi had made herself a small breakfast.

"Guess I didn't have to tell you to make yourself at home," Boon joked.

"Shiiit. I hope you didn't think I was going to sit in here and starve. Besides, I made you some too. It's on the stove." CiCi said. Boon shook his head and smiled. "So, what they tell you about ya wifey?" CiCi asked.

Boon went into the kitchen, warming his food in the microwave. CiCi had made omelets, cheese grits, turkey bacon, and Boon made his own toast. As the microwave hummed, Boon said, "Nothin' really. Do I know anyone that may have wanted to hurt her? Where was I? You know, the usual," Boon replied.

"Well, do you know anybody that wanted to hurt her?" CiCi asked.

Boon emerged from the kitchen, with his steaming hot plate of food in his hand, and joined CiCi on the couch.

"It's funny you should ask that question," Boon said, and CiCi thought she was busted. "They showed me a video message that pissed me off. The video of...of her fuckin' this dude I used to be friends with. I remember his wife sending me the same video, but she told me I owe her some dick and all kinds of crazy shit. Hell, she might've done that shit," Boon said, throwing his head back to bless his food.

CiCi shook her head, surprised that Boon, the sharp lawyer, hadn't figured it out yet.

"They said she was killed how, again?" CiCi probed.

"They say with a..." Boon looked at CiCi. "What kind of gun is that you got, Curelle?" Boon asked, suspiciously.

"One big enough to bust a ho shit apart," she smartly answered.

"Girl, what kind—"

"A .45, Daniel. Damn!" CiCi cut in.

Boon's jaw dropped. "You?" he mustered. CiCi only nodded. "Why?" Boon had to know.

"She was causin' you grief and I knew it. She pulled a gun on me. She tried to make me look bad when you married her. That bitch was getting away with murder, so I tried to get away with it too. Pun intended," CiCi said, without so much as a nervous twitch.

Boon was shocked. He knew CiCi would swing on a bitch without hesitation, but trigger play was a different game. Boon, still at a loss for words, stared into CiCi's eyes. CiCi, slyly, returned his gaze.

"What?" she said.

"I'm shocked. I mean, I know you a fighter, but you blew Amerie's head the fuck off." Boon opened his hands and spread his arms to demonstrate the explosion of Amerie's cranium. CiCi sucked her teeth.

"Man, fuck that bird, with much disrespect!" she yelled.

Boon was about to say something else, but was interrupted by the ringing of his phone.

"Hello?" he answered, after recognizing it was his dad calling him.

"Daniel, Cook County Police just left here looking for you. They found three of your ex-girlfriends dead and want to speak wit'cha about them. Right now, you aren't a suspect, but the detectives say if you don't come see them within the next 48 hours, you will be," Daylon said, with little emphasis.

"Say no more, Pop. I'm on the way." Boon told his dad.

"Son," Daylon spoke and stopped Boon from hanging up. "…have you talked to Curelle?" he asked.

Boon smiled. "Yeah, I have, Pop. And I already know." Boon rubbed CiCi's thigh.

"Glad to hear. So, we'll see you soon then?" Daylon quizzed.

"Most def. Most def." Boon replied, before he hung up the phone.

"So, what's up?" CiCi asked.

Boon stood up and stretched. "We gotta go. I need to see what the po-po want wit' a nigga back home. More importantly, I wanna see my son," Boon said.

CiCi got up, kissed Boon's lips, and prepared for their departure.

Boon urged CiCi to leave the rental in the driveway and ride back to Chi-Town with him in the Tahoe.

"Baby girl, you drive. I need to make a couple phone calls right quick," Boon requested.

They jumped in and Boon made the call to the Cook County Police Department. He told them he was en route and there wasn't a need for warrants. The officer then put Boon on the line with the lead detective on the case. The lead detective informed him that, as of now, he was only a person of interest, and just needed to come and answer a few questions. Boon ended the call and cut the radio on. He and CiCi had a long trip ahead of them.

*

Boon and CiCi finally reached Cook County PD at 8 in the evening. They were both exhausted from the adventure, but were ready to get this situation behind them.

"So," CiCi began, as she opened the driver's door of the truck to get out. "...let's get this show on the road."

Boon nodded, sliding out of the Tahoe. Boon exhaled a strong breath and joined CiCi on the march to the police station. As Boon looked at

CiCi, he was grateful she was there with him. They had been friends for next to forever, and through everything, here she was, still hanging tough.

Boon held the door open for CiCi and followed her into the station.

"I'm here to speak with Detective Gaston," Boon said to the heavyset, bald-headed officer working the desk. His nameplate read: **Thompson**.

"Name?" Officer Thompson barked.

"Daniel Watson. Attorney Daniel Watson." Boon showed his driver's license.

Officer Thompson pointed in the direction of the detectives' area. Boon walked over and was met at the desk by a tall and muscular black guy. He was wearing a pair of black slacks, a green, button-down shirt, and instead of a tie, his badge swung from his neck.

"May I help you?" He greeted Boon, and reached his hand out for a shake.

"I'm Daniel Watson. You needed to see me?"

The detective smiled and shook hands with Boon. "Follow me. Your guest can wait here," Detective Gaston told Boon.

Boon looked at CiCi and told her, "I'll be back, beautiful."

Boon followed the detective to what would be his second interrogation room in as many days. And again, he wasn't there as a defense attorney. Boon took a seat, as did Detective Gaston. The detective had a manila folder in his hand that he sat on the table.

Mr. Watson, are you familiar with an Ebony Charles of West Chicago?" the detective asked, as he peered into the folder.

"Yes, sir. I am," Boon said.

"She was found dead in her apartment by her cousin two days ago. Know anything about that?" Detective Gaston looked at Boon.

"No, sir. I mean, why would I?" Boon didn't mean to sound like he was being a smart-ass, but the detective did take it that way.

"You were her ex-boyfriend and she's dead now," the detective said louder.

Boon sat back in his chair. "Coincidental," he said, simply.

"I thought that, too, at first. That is... until… " the detective paused, as he pulled out three photos. "… we came across these three cadavers. Giovanni Frazier, Jamela Howard, Tatiyana Lopes, and this here unlucky guy we found with Ms. Howard." Gaston pulled out a fourth photo of a dickless Yo.

Boon shook his head in disgust. "And these pictures have exactly what to do with me?" Boon's uninterested tone was flat.

The detective looked at Boon, as if he wanted to slap him.

"So, you mean to tell me, we find four of your exes and an old friend of yours dead in the same week, and you have not a single thing to do with it? No clue or nothing?" Gaston spoke in utter disbelief.

Boon was skilled at this game. He had to school many clients on police scare tactics, and being on the receiving end was a joke.

"That's exactly what I'm telling you. I've been out of touch with those people for a long, and I do mean, a very long time. Now, unless you got something to charge me with, I should be free to go," Boon said.

"I don't think so," Gaston said, pulling another piece of paper out of the folder. "We got a missing person's report on a Zora Tucker, who also happens to be an ex of yours." The detective sat the paper on the table, face-up. "And," he began again, "we also spoke with Harris County PD. Your wife was killed two days ago."

Boon smirked. "Look, all this sounds like you are doing your job very well, Detective

Gaston, but I still didn't do anything. My wife was killed while I was on my way home from here. These people, I haven't even seen in at least a year, or longer." Boon was pointing to the photos on the table in front of him, emphasizing his point.

"You got somebody to vouch for your whereabouts on the days in question?" Detective Gaston asked, but he already knew the answer. Boon's facial expression showed they shared the same sentiment.

"I came up to visit my parents, which is still legal. They can verify for you where I was. And Harris County PD should've told you that they also got the proof they were looking for. Sorry, Detective, but you got the wrong guy." Boon shrugged his shoulders.

The detective looked on, pissed off, but had nothing he could hold Boon for any longer. "A'ight. A'ight. You on top of shit right now. But you better not fart where I can smell it, or you gonna wear these homicides," he hissed, as he stood from his seat.

Boon stood as well, locking eyes with the detective. "Man, save all that *New York Undercover* bullshit for one of these youngsters. And if you close enough to smell me fartin', then you need counseling and a muthafuckin'

girlfriend, Detective. Good evening to you, sir."
Boon walked out of the interrogation room and
back to the desk where they'd left CiCi. "Let's
go, baby girl," Boon said to CiCi, as he walked
past.

"Catch ya later, homeboy," Boon heard
Gaston say from behind him. Boon threw up the
deuces, without looking back, and walked out of
the police station.

"So, you gon' tell me what it look like?"
CiCi was curious about what they'd asked Boon,
but he had been quiet for most of the ride.

They were now 15 minutes away from his
parents' house. Boon turned and looked at CiCi,
who was driving.

"They showed me pictures of all of them
dirty bitches. Wanted to know if I knew
anything," Boon chuckled. "I know I'm glad
they triflin'-asses is through."

"What about this Amerie situation? What am
I looking at?" CiCi quizzed.

Boon wasn't about to lose her. Not now.
"You know I got you. Yo' crazy-ass. We gotta
stay in Houston though. I'm through wit' Chi-
Raq." Boon referred to Chicago by its insulting,
yet well-earned, nickname.

CiCi laughed. "I miss kickin' it wit' you like
this. My nigga, Boon."

Curelle parked the truck on the side of the curb and shut off the engine.

"Boon, I want to ask you a very serious question." CiCi took off her seatbelt and turned slightly to face Boon in the passenger seat. Boon did the same. "Can I get a fair shot? I mean, a fair shot at being yours. No bullshit, bitches, or tryna kill me?" CiCi smirked a little.

Boon laughed. "I would actually love that. Just don't be holdin' out on me wit' da pussy, Curelle. You know I'm a Scorpio. I be needin' that shit like oxygen." Both Boon and CiCi laughed.

After sharing a kiss, Curelle looked at Boon and said, "Now, let's go see your big-headed son."

Deysha Vu

Boon and CiCi walked into Boon's parents' house hand in hand, just as they'd done so many times in high school.

"Boy, brang yo'self over here and look at yo' twin," Boon's mom called over to him. She was holding three-month-old Dietrich and feeding him. Boon's palms began to sweat and he was nauseous. Sensing this, CiCi put her hand in the small of his back and walked him to where his mother sat with his son. "Ain't no need in you getting all sickly on us now. My grandbaby gon' need you to hold all that together."

Boon gathered himself, wiped his hand across his face, then said, "Lemme see him, Mama."

Mrs. Watson sat up and handed his son to an emotional Boon.

After spending an hour talking to and playing with Dietrich, the little guy was all tuckered out. Boon laid him in his bassinet for a nap.

"So, baby daddy," CiCi rubbed Boon's back. "I need a...a good slaying right now."

Boon turned to face Curelle, "Oh yeah?" he said, with the sly grin she knew and loved.

"You take that in your room, son. I'll keep an eye on the youngster," Daylon said, coming out of the restroom.

Boon took him up on the offer and went to his room, with CiCi in tow.

Boon and CiCi had a blissful lovemaking session, during which CiCi shed tears of pure joy. They went to get Dietrich after Daylon told them he and Mrs. Watson had to step out for a moment. The baby was still sleep, however, so Boon activated the baby monitor, and he and CiCi went downstairs.

Boon, beginning to unwind a bit, decided to make a light dinner. No sooner than he'd vanished into the kitchen, Deysha came through the front door. She looked like she had seen better days. She sat her purse and her keys down.

"What you doin' here?" she barked, snaking her neck at CiCi. CiCi rolled her eyes at Deysha. Boon had just dicked her down properly, and she wasn't in the mood for any of Deysha's jealous, sibling bullshit. "Oh, so you can't hear?" Deysha took off her earrings.

"So, you really tryna do that shit here?" CiCi stood up. "Let's go outside, bitch!" CiCi said.

She wasn't about to let Deysha disrespect her, period. Deysha moved in on her, instead of going out the door. CiCi didn't hesitate. She gave her a swift right hook, followed with a straight left, and yet another hard right hook. As Deysha stumbled backwards, she grabbed a crystal candy dish from the coffee table and hit a charging CiCi in the face with it. CiCi had to step back and regroup from the blow. By this time, Boon burst into the room to see what all of the commotion was about. When he saw Deysha's bloodied lip and Curelle holding her jaw, he knew what it was.

"Man, what the fuck is wrong with y'all?" he scowled. "Deysha, what the fuck?" Boon yelled; he was heated.

Before Deysha or CiCi could answer, Dietrich's crying sounded off through the baby monitor receiver.

"My baby!" CiCi rushed up the stairs to tend to her little one.

"Boon, you think you slick." Deysha's eyes were swollen from CiCi's vicious blows.

"Fuck is you talkin' 'bout?" Boon screamed.

"I know what you did, nigga. You runnin' around, got everybody feeling sorry for you, 'cause your choice in women ain't shit. It's your fault my husband left me and my son alone. You're just as bad as the bitches you killed, Daniel." Deysha was hysterical.

"What could I possibly have to do with your husband leaving you alone? The nigga probably left 'cause he realized you a crazy bitch!" Boon matched her tone.

"He said we were too close to just be brother and sister, said he believes I've fucked you before." Deysha's eyes were watering.

Boon looked confused. "What? You're my damn sister. That's fuckin' ridiculous, Mae."

"No. What's ridiculous is, maybe he saw something. I love you more than I should; and now that he's gone, I won't let that bitch upstairs take you away from me too. No way in hell!" Deysha went to her purse when she saw CiCi come down the stairs.

"Oh, you a nasty broad. I knew it had to be somethin' wit' you goin' the extra mile to get all ya brother's bitches away from him!" CiCi chimed in.

Deysha spun around with a chrome .38 in her hand.

"Deysha, what the hell is that for?" Boon asked.

"Either that ho leaves you to me, or she gon' leave, period!" Deysha let the tears fall.

"C'mon, Mae, you and I... we... you my fuckin' *sister*, man. You know ain't shit can happen!" Boon stood between the gun and its target - CiCi.

"Boon, you're too good for these hoes. That baby may not be yours either. You know I wouldn't hurt you though," Deysha sobbed.

"Mae, c'mon, sis, let me have the gun. It ain't helpin' the conversation at all right now." Boon extended his arms, still short of the .38's range.

"No, Boon. I can't leave you. This ol' conceited-ass ho don't deserve you." She side-stepped him and aimed at CiCi again.

Boon charged her and grabbed the gun, but Deysha's grip was nearly inhuman. She and Boon struggled with the gun, as Deysha squeezed off two, consecutive shots that went through the ceiling. CiCi ran upstairs to grab her .45. She hadn't allowed Amerie to get away with drawing down on her, and neither could Deysha. She didn't give a fuck about her being Boon's sister. She heard the gun go off twice more. When she got downstairs, she saw Boon lying down on his side, but he had the gun. Deysha was standing over him, covering her mouth with her hands.

"Bitch, you gotta die!" CiCi let off a round in Deysha's thigh. "You sick, twisted-ass bitch!"

CiCi was about to shoot again, but she stopped when she heard Boon's wavering voice. "Nooooo..." he stated, weakly, as he staggered to his feet.

"Boon, I'm finna kill this ho. We can't both be a part of your life. She want the thing she definitely can't have, and we see how far she willing to go to get that!" CiCi aimed at the back of Deysha's head.

Deysha was frozen, stock-still; she was in shock. She really did love her brother, but wanted more from him than a brother could offer a sister.

"Curelle!" Boon hollered, "Call me a fuckin' ambulance. Now!" CiCi lowered her gun and ran to the kitchen. She came back with the cordless phone, as she dialed 911. "Tell them two guys came in to try to rob us and shot me and Deysha. Go put these fuckin' guns away!" Boon instructed.

He had been shot in the side and in his thigh, and he had lost a substantial amount of blood. Deysha collapsed beside him, when her wound caused her to drop.

*

Before the ambulance arrived, Boon coached the women through the story. Boon was able to get his sister calm enough to agree to the plan and to keep quiet about his murderous spree of axing exes.

"You two were very lucky," the EMT said to Boon and Deysha. "Between where you were hit and what you were hit with, most don't come out living."

CiCi visited Boon every day, until he was released from the hospital. She even put aside Deysha's maniacal behavior from the day she shot Boon, and visited her too. As it turned the girl had been suffering from a chemical imbalance that had gone untreated for years. Her parents had always written it off as her being overly dramatic, but she was suffering from bipolar disorder. It was another case of mental illness being swept under the rug instead of treated and it had almost cost Boon and Cici their lives. The doctors assured her that so long as Deysha stayed on her meds it was lessen the chances of another mental break. For the sake of Boon, Cici would forgive her, but she'd never forget.

The three of them sat in Grace, an upscale restaurant on W. Randolph Street in Chicago, sharing a meal. Dietrich was with his Uncle Drakus, picking up chicks.

"Man, I love y'all two. Real shit," Boon confessed to CiCi and Deysha.

"Aww, I love you too, baby," CiCi said, with mush all in her tone.

Deysha nodded. "Me three, baby bruh." She added, "I never got to apologize for my actions, you two."

Boon waved his hand in dismissal. "Yeah, that was some crazy shit, but we good now. So long as you stick to them meds."

"I think we all learned lessons in this whole mess, and hopefully we can grow from them." CiCi chimed in.

"I know I did." Boon took Cici's hand in his. "I was looking for love in all the wrong places, but the whole time it was right under my nose."

MORE TITLES FROM WRITE 2 EAT CONCEPTS

THINK OUTSIDE THE BOX...WRITE OUTSIDE THE LINES